OCTOBER MOON

A journey from apparent normality through fear, then terror, *October Moon* ends in full-blown horror. A terrifying excursion into the unknown from the pen of a master storyteller.

'Scott's grasp of the macabre and his confident moving between reality and fantasy provide a suitably scary fiction for dark evenings'

Robert Dunbar, THE IRISH TIMES

An exciting series from
THE O'BRIEN PRESS

October Moon is the first title in this thrilling series, bringing you the best in fantasy, horror, magic, the supernatural and science fiction, from new as well as well-known writers. See next page for other titles in the series.

Watch ... ooks,

Michael Scott

Born and brought up in Dublin, Michael Scott worked in a variety of bookshops, and was an antiquarian bookseller before turning to writing as a fulltime activity. First published in 1981, he has written and published approximately fifty books to date. Married, with two children, he lives in Dublin.

Michael Scott's books for young readers include stories from Celtic mythology, fairytales and fantasy, horror and the supernatural.

The *Irish Guide to Children's Books* praised Michael Scott for his 'unparalleled contribution to children's literature'.

OTHER WORLD TITLES

October Moon

Gemini Game

House of the Dead

(all by Michael Scott)

Moonlight, by Michael Carroll

OCTOBER MOON

Michael Scott

THE O'BRIEN PRESS
DUBLIN

First published 1992 by The O'Brien Press Ltd.,
20 Victoria Road, Rathgar, Dublin 6, Ireland.
This edition published 1993.

British Library Cataloguing-in-publication Data
A catalogue reference for this title is available
from the British Library.

10 9 8 7 6 5 4 3 2

ISBN 0–86278–300-3

The O'Brien Press receives assistance from
The Arts Council/An Chomhairle Ealaíon

Cover illustration: Peter Haigh
Cover design: Neasa Ní Chianáin
Typesetting, layout and design: The O'Brien Press
Printing: Cox & Wyman Ltd., Reading

for the real
Piers de Courtney...

What evil wakes,
What shadows walk,
What creatures skulk,
What horror stalks,
Beneath the October Moon

Sunday, 25th October

Prologue

THE SHADOWY FIGURE CROUCHED in the musty, straw-filled barn. A match rasped and hissed alight.

The tiny red winking eye slowly spiralled downwards onto the dry straw, where it flared then vanished. A heartbeat later, a tendril of white smoke curled upwards and then the first yellow flame danced along the golden straw.

The fire took hold with frightening rapidity, eating into the straw dried by a long hot summer, and within moments flames were crackling through the hay barn.

The flames and grey-white smoke drove the figure back through the half-open doors. It turned, sliding home the heavy bolt even as smoke was streaming out from beneath the door, and then stood back.

There was a dull roaring sound from within the building. Smoke was now seeping from every crack in the wood, drifting straight up into the clear night sky. Wood suddenly snapped and shattered, the three small windows exploding with the intense heat. The barn's double doors slowly twisted and pulled from their hinges as the fire ate through them.

When it was satisfied that the barn couldn't be saved, the figure slunk away from the building and darted across the moon-bright fields. It paused once, in the shadow of an ancient oak tree and looked back at the destruction it had caused, and then it threw back its head and howled in triumph.

Monday, 26th October

1

IT TOOK A MOMENT FOR RACHEL STONE to make sense of what she was seeing. She leaned forward and pressed the button that lowered the window, allowing chill, earth-scented air into the car's warm interior.

"Dad?" she whispered.

Robert Stone looked up from the report he was reading. He followed his daughter's pointing finger and swore softly. He leaned forward and tapped on the glass partition separating him from the driver. "Stop here."

The uniformed driver immediately pulled the sleek black limousine off the road onto the grass verge and stopped. Before he could get out to open the doors for his passengers, Robert Stone had leapt from the car and was striding across the fields towards the still-smouldering ruin of a barn. Rachel reached over and gently shook her mother awake. "Mom, I think you should look at this."

"What's wrong?" Elizabeth Stone asked sleepily, but Rachel had already climbed out of the car. With a sigh, the older woman followed her daughter, pressing her hands in the small of her back, stiff after the long drive from Dublin airport. "Oh," she said quietly.

Rachel pulled a pair of Ray Ban sun-glasses from the top of her head and slid them on. The autumnal sunshine slanting in low across the fields made her eyes water. "Did you know about this, Mom?" she asked, shading her eyes with her hands.

"We got a call last night," Elizabeth said quietly. "Your father wanted to cancel the trip."

"I was wondering what had put him in such a foul humour.

He's barely spoken since we left the airport."

"I think he's fed up with this place. So far, it's been nothing but trouble." Elizabeth Stone turned and climbed back into the car, settling on the soft leather seats, and pulled an orange juice from the well-stocked bar. Rachel climbed in beside her, pushing her sun-glasses back onto her head, blinking in the car's dim interior. She rubbed her hands together. It was actually quite cool outside; back home in California she'd still be wearing light summer clothes. "What happened?" she asked.

Her mother shrugged. "Accident, I suppose."

The two women were often taken for sisters, although Rachel was fifteen and her mother twenty years older. They had the same honey-blond hair, though while Rachel's colouring was natural, her mother's came out of a bottle. They had flawless skin, perfect tans, brilliantly white teeth, long, almost oval faces and bright blue eyes.

"I wouldn't be at all surprised if your Dad's thinking of selling this place," Elizabeth said softly, sipping her drink.

"But we've only bought it," Rachel protested, peering through the open door at the flat undulating Irish countryside. "Ever since I was a child, Dad has talked about owning a stud on the Curragh in Ireland."

"There have been too many accidents," her mother said. She nodded at the smouldering remains of the barn. "This is the last straw." Both woman smiled at the unintentional joke.

Rachel watched her father pick through the barn. He stopped to talk to a blue-uniformed police officer. His arms were waving and she guessed that his famous temper was bubbling up to boiling point.

She knew how excited her father had been when the stud had come up for sale in Ireland. She had come home from high school and found the brochure sitting on top of the television. She remembered opening it, turning it around to look at the small rectangular colour photograph of a house and stables. Her father had scrawled his accountant's number across the bottom of the brochure ... and she knew then that he was going to buy it, no matter what the price.

She remembered how excited she had been at the prospect of actually coming to Ireland. Irish horses were considered amongst the best in the world, and the Curragh had an international reputation for its stables and training yards.

The Stones were third generation horse breeders. Robert's grandfather had started breeding horses just before the First World War. He made his fortune during the war when the animals were used for carrying supplies across countryside where no wheeled vehicle could pass. Robert's father had built upon the fortune and had started breeding and racing thoroughbreds. Robert and Elizabeth had met as members of the American Olympics dressage team in 1968. They had married two years later. They were now considered to be amongst the top ten horse breeders in the world, with two large stud farms on the West Coast of America, another in Texas, and two more in Argentina and Australia.

"This is the third fire in less than a month," Elizabeth Stone muttered. "And two weeks ago, Sheikh Nazir's prize stallion was found on the grounds with its throat cut."

Rachel felt bile flood her mouth. "Who would do that?" she whispered.

"Maybe the same people who would burn down a barn," her mother suggested.

Rachel Stone pulled the door closed and sat back into the seat. Suddenly the Irish countryside didn't seem so welcoming anymore.

Seasonstown House had originally been built at the end of the sixteenth century. Over the next four hundred years it had been burnt out and rebuilt, then demolished and rebuilt once more before it was finally allowed to fall into disrepair as the last owner of the house gambled away a fortune on the gaming tables in Monte Carlo. In the nineteen seventies, it had been bought by a retired jockey and partially refitted as a stud farm. The horses he trained had won several races, but the jockey's extravagant life-style eventually cost him everything.

Rachel's first impression of the sprawling building was that it looked unfinished. Two wings had been built at slight angles onto the main body of the house. The place was a mixture of styles and materials, with three different-coloured slates on the roof and two contrasting red bricks; the windows in the right-hand wing were in a completely different style to the rest of the house, while all the windows in the left-hand wing had been bricked up.

"How much did you pay for this, Dad?" she wondered aloud.

Robert Stone grinned. "Bit of a disaster isn't it? I really bought the land and the stud; the house came more or less free."

"I'm not surprised."

"Mind you, with a bit of money and some clever restoration, it would be worth a few dollars. It might be a nice place to retire to," he added, winking at his daughter.

"Make a nice hotel," she said absently.

Robert turned to look through the window again, sweeping his blond hair off his forehead with a quick nervous movement. He nodded briefly. The house would make a nice hotel. He made a mental note to have one of his accountants work out the costs for a project like that.

The limousine swept up a long gravelled driveway, slowed and then stopped before broad stone steps. The double doors immediately opened and three women and two men appeared.

With the exception of one of the men, they were all wearing what looked like a crude attempt at a servant's uniform: blue skirts and cardigans over white blouses for the women, blue trousers and matching jacket for the man. One of the group hurried down the steps. He was wearing a tweed jacket, yellow polo neck jumper, jodphurs and gleaming black riding boots. When he took off his cap, Rachel was surprised to discover that he was completely bald, although she guessed that he was only in his late twenties. He pulled open the car door and reached for Robert's hand as he climbed out of the car.

"Sean Summers, Sir. It's good to meet you at last."

Robert Stone shook hands with the soft-spoken Irishman. He had only ever spoken to Summers on the phone, and he was surprised to discover that he was so young. Yet he came highly recommended as one of the best estate managers in the country.

"This is my wife, Elizabeth, and my daughter, Rachel," he completed the introductions.

"A great pleasure to meet you all. Welcome to Ireland. I hope you have a very happy stay here."

Robert jerked his thumb over his shoulder in the general direction of the burnt-out barn. "Not a great introduction."

"No, Sir," Summers admitted.

"Accident ...?" Robert asked.

"The police are inclined to think otherwise."

"Deliberate then. Arson; but why?"

Summers shook his head. "I don't know, Sir."

"We'll talk about it later."

"Yes, Sir," Summers said, obviously relieved to be moving away from the difficult topic. "The staff have come out to meet you and Mrs Stone, and Miss Rachel of course," he added, turning to smile at her. Rachel decided in that moment that she didn't particularly like the man. Two of the women's names were in what Rachel assumed was the Irish language and so she didn't even make an attempt to remember them. The old man, who seemed to be a gardener and general handyman was called Paddy, and the youngest staff member, a girl of roughly her own age, was called Agnes.

It smelt dry and musty inside the house, like a room that has been kept locked for too long. The hallway was broad, decorated in a pattern of black and white tiles, and a magnificent staircase faced the doors, polished wood gleaming in the late afternoon sunshine.

"It looks like something out of a movie," Elizabeth muttered.

One of the older women led them up the stairs. "It's so nice to have someone living in the house again."

"How long was it locked up?" Elizabeth asked, looking around.

"It's been nearly a year since poor Mr Allen died," she said, and Rachel was surprised to see her cross herself.

"Did you work for Tommy Allen?" Robert asked, trailing his hand along the banister. The wood was smooth, polished to a light golden colour. He wondered if it was oak.

"I did, Sir. Did you know Mr Allen then?"

"I did. He rode some of my father's horses. He was a great jockey."

The woman nodded. "So I've heard, Sir." She stopped at a panelled door. "This is the master bedroom. You and Mrs Stone will be in here." She pushed open the door and moved back, allowing Robert and Elizabeth to step into the room. Rachel followed them. The room was enormous. A fireplace took up one wall and four floor-to-ceiling windows took up another. "The bathroom is through here," the woman continued, opening a door to the right of the bed. Rachel had been

15

expecting an ancient-looking bathroom, but instead she found herself looking into a bright, rather stark room, complete with shower and bidet.

"I've put you in the room at the other end of the landing, Miss Rachel," the woman said, walking out of the room. Rachel hesitated for a moment, then followed her. "It used to be a guest room. Mr Allen always had guests staying. Will you have many guests, do you think?" she asked abruptly.

"I'm not even sure if we'll be staying ourselves," Rachel said quickly.

The bedroom wasn't as big as her parents', but it was still large. It had been decorated in a mixture of gold and white and the overall effect was rather overpowering. An enormous fireplace, almost big enough to stand up in, took up one wall and the two large windows looked out over the back of the house, onto the stables. The en-suite bathroom was also decorated in yellow and white; even the taps were gold. There was a big mirror over the bath.

"Are all the bedrooms like this?" Rachel asked.

The woman paused by the door. "No, Miss," she admitted. "I've given you the two best rooms. All the other rooms on this floor are slightly smaller, and Mr Allen never did get around to decorating those on the floor above. I'll have your cases sent up," she added, closing the door behind her.

Rachel looked around the room again. She was pleasantly surprised. From the exterior of the building, she'd imagined something dim and dingy. She flopped down on the bed ... and immediately bounced off again as the whole lot rippled beneath her. She poked it with her forefinger, and it quivered like jelly. It was a water-bed! She prodded the bed again, and it shivered like a balloon.

The girl crossed to the nearest window and looked out. She was looking down onto the famous Seasonstown Stables. She counted forty-eight individual stalls, most of which seemed to be occupied. The yard was busy, with horses coming and going. She spotted Sean Summers and a smaller man in a white coat, whom she guessed was a vet, standing beside a huge mountain of golden hay. The two men were deep in conversation.

A red-haired stable-girl appeared, holding the reins on a magnificent night-black stallion. She spoke briefly to Summers before leading the animal into one of the stalls. Before she disappeared, she stopped and raised her head to look up at the bedroom window. Rachel jerked her head back.

There was an expression of pure hatred on the girl's face!

2

THIRTEEN PEOPLE WERE GATHERED in the bare room. There were no lights lit and none were needed.

The young woman made her report quickly. "They've come. The man, the woman and the girl."

"Will they stay?" The voice was old, wheezing, every word an effort.

"For a while."

"They must stay," the wheezing voice insisted. "Make them stay, they must live in the house ... at least until the Hallows Eve. Then we'll be free."

"Free," the other twelve whispered together, the sound like a great indrawn breath. "Free."

"They'll stay," the young woman promised, "until the Hallows Eve, the October Moon."

Tuesday, 27th October

3

RACHEL STOPPED OUTSIDE the dining room door and pressed the heels of her hands against her eyes, then ran her fingers through her hair, pulling it back off her face. She felt dreadful. A combination of jet-lag, an incredibly uncomfortable night on the shifting water-bed, and a vivid nightmare that had brought her awake cold and shivering in the early hours of the morning left her feeling numb and exhausted.

She peered around the door. The sun was shining in through the long windows and French doors and the room was bright and cheerful. The light was so sharp it brought tears to her eyes. Her father was alone at the table, reading the morning newspaper over a cup of coffee. He raised his head as she stepped into the room, took one look at the expression on her face and put down the paper. "You look ill." As she came around to kiss his forehead, he pressed the back of his hand to her cheek, then felt her forehead. "You're not hot though."

Rachel stared at the plate of fried egg, bacon and something which looked like thick black sausage and felt her stomach do a quick tumble. She pushed the plate away in case she threw up, grabbed the orange juice, drank it in one long swallow and immediately refilled the glass.

"What's wrong, sweetheart?"

"There's a water-bed in my room," she said simply.

Robert stared at her blankly.

"Every time I moved, ripples ran up and down it. Even when I didn't move, it rippled. I dreamt about standing on the deck of a heaving yacht at sea. I dreamt I was seasick." She looked at her father with her bright blue eyes, daring him to laugh. "I feel seasick."

Robert looked down at the newspaper again, not meeting her eyes.

"I know you think it's funny," she continued.

He shook his head, his eyes fixed on his coffee, but she could see that his shoulders were shaking.

Elizabeth Stone strode into the small circular dining room. "Good morning. Smell that air!" She sat down and looked at Robert and Rachel. "What's the matter with you two?" She stopped and stared hard at her daughter. "You look ill."

Robert snorted.

Rachel glared at her father for a moment, then she too began to laugh. Elizabeth stared at them blankly. "What have I missed?" she wondered.

"Rachel dreamt herself seasick," Robert laughed.

"There's a water-bed in my room."

"Oh, is that all! There's not enough water in it," Elizabeth said immediately, surprising them both into silence. "It just needs to be topped up to make it firmer. It won't roll so easily then." She shrugged. "Pass the toast." She looked up to see her husband and daughter staring at her. "I used to have a water-bed," she explained. "Drink some sweet tea. It will help settle your stomach."

They ate in silence for a while, Rachel cautiously sipping the tea, feeling the greasy queasiness gradually fade away. She wasn't sure what had made her feel so nauseous: the water-bed or the nightmare. She dreamt that she had been standing on the heaving deck of a ship at sea. Waves were washing in over the sides, tossing objects onto the deck which crawled away when she turned to look at them. She remembered turning around and around and discovering that the deck was on fire, but she couldn't get off the ship. When she tried to throw herself off, a huge wave would toss her back onto the burning deck. Just before she woke up the ship had transformed into a burning barn. But when she tried to leave the smoke-filled barn, a vague shape would catch her and spin her back into it.

"You should go for a ride," her mother said suddenly, startling her. "That will help clear your head."

"Good idea," Robert added. "Ask Summers's advice about an animal and a trail. Did you bring your boots and hat?"

Rachel smiled, the last remnants of the nightmare drifting away with the thoughts of choosing a horse and going for a ride. "Of course, Dad. You don't think I was going to come to Ireland and not go riding?"

Rachel found Sean Summers in the stables, examining a snow-white gelding. She stood in the doorway, watching the man run his hands across the horse's flanks, his fingers probing muscles and joints. She was about to step into the bright, airy stable when the tall red-haired girl she had seen from her window appeared. The two young women stared at one another. Rachel attempted to return the other girl's fixed and unblinking stare, but found she had to drop her eyes. The red-haired girl stepped up to Summers and muttered something. The estate manager straightened up and turned around.

"Ah, Miss Stone. Good morning to you. And a good morning for a ride too," he added, noting her riding boots and hard hat.

"Good morning, Mr Summers. I didn't wish to disturb you ..."

"You're not disturbing me. I've was just looking over The Ghost." He patted the white horse's flanks and nodded at the red-haired girl. "Maeve tells me he had a restless night."

Rachel glanced at the girl; she was still staring with the same

22

fixed, venomous expression, but she quickly looked away, tilting her head to one side to look at the animal. "I think he's favouring his right foreleg," Rachel said.

Summers looked at her, then ran the palm of his hand down the beast's leg. It whickered. "You're right," he said admiringly. "It's bruised."

"Probably reared up and kicked it off the stall," Rachel said.

"You're right. Take him down to the vet, just in case," Summers said to the red-haired girl. As she led the animal away, he turned back to Rachel. "You know your animals, Miss."

She laughed. "I learned to ride before I could walk, Mr Summers. I hope to ride in the '96 Olympics."

Summers looked impressed. "It's nice to get someone who knows horses. I mean really knows them," he added. "Some people now, they just look on a stables as another investment, but your father, he really loves horses."

"We all do, Mr Summers. Now," she continued, "I'd like to choose a horse. What would you recommend?"

Summers pulled his cap off and rubbed his hand across his bald head before setting the cap back in place. "If you're that experienced a rider, you could take your pick of the mounts."

"I saw a magnificent black yesterday ..." She pointed across the yard. "That stall, I think."

He smiled quickly, showing yellow crooked teeth. "That would be Oiche." He pronounced it *Ee-ha*. "That's the Irish word for night. A two-year-old filly. A good choice," he added. "Normally, I wouldn't allow anyone but the jockey to ride her, but since you're such an experienced rider ... I'll get you a saddle."

Rachel wandered around the stables while Summers went to fetch a saddle. She was aware that the red-haired girl was watching her closely. Rachel guessed she would be roughly

23

around her own age, but she was tall and broad, thick ridges of muscle showing in her bare forearms. She was obviously incredibly strong. Her skin was almost unnaturally white, splotched with freckles and her deep-sunk bright green eyes seemed to burn in her face. Against her pale skin, her mane of bright red hair seemed even more vivid. It was pulled back off her face, tied into a crude pony tail that hung almost to the base of her spine. Rachel knew girls back home who would kill for hair like that.

Rachel walked the length of the stables, breathing in the rich aroma of straw, horse flesh and manure. She knew some people found it disgusting, but she had grown up with the smell, and always associated it with happy memories.

Summers reappeared carrying a saddle over his shoulder. "What do you think of the place?" he asked.

"I'm very impressed," she said, falling into step beside him.

Summers waited while Rachel unlatched Oiche's stall, then he slipped in past her, talking quietly to the night-black animal. Rachel walked up to the horse, allowing it to smell her. She produced half an apple from her coat pocket which the filly snatched with a neat, precise movement of her head, whickering her enjoyment.

As Summers cinched the saddle and adjusted the stirrups, Rachel expertly slid the bridle over the horse's head, sliding the bit into place.

"Oiche's strong and fast," he said, "but you have to show her who's boss. Give her her head; she loves a gallop, but make sure you stay in charge."

Rachel rubbed the palm of her hand down the horse's neck. "I will."

Summers cupped his hands and helped the girl vault up into the saddle. He stood back, brushing off his hands. "You look like you belong up there," he grinned. Then his smile faded. "Do you think your father will keep this place, Miss?" When Rachel didn't immediately reply, he continued quickly, "I mean, we've heard rumours that he might be selling it. And I don't suppose the accidents have helped."

"My father loves horses, Mr Summers," Rachel said cautiously. "He's been looking for a place like this in Ireland for as long as I can remember. I don't know what he's going to do, but I don't think he'll give it up without a fight."

Summers nodded quickly, realising that he wasn't going to get any more from the girl. "Follow the track out onto the Curragh, Miss. Enjoy yourself. And don't forget, if you get lost, just ask for Seasonstown House. Anyone will show you the way."

Rachel Stone walked the filly from the yard, enjoying being back in the saddle again. Back home in the States, she rode every day, often three or four times a day during the holidays. She had two horses of her own: Scarecrow and Tin Man, both named after characters from her favourite book. She missed them now and wondered if the staff were taking good care of them.

Once beyond the yard she allowed Oiche to canter. She moved easily with the horse across the flat rolling countryside, breathing in the cool, clean morning air. There were a few clouds on the horizon, and just the touch of a chill breeze reminding her that this was October, but the day promised to be fine.

She stopped once, standing in the saddle to look all around her. Despite the gold and russets of the autumnal foliage, the landscape was so green, the colours so vibrant they almost hurt her eyes. In the States, the predominant colours were brown and gold, and on the estate in Australia, the colours were dusty ochres and reds.

A dark speck on the landscape attracted her attention, and

she turned Oiche's head towards it. Digging her heels in, she urged the horse to a gallop, feeling the power that trembled up through the animal's back, the ground thundering by beneath its hooves. From what she knew of horses, this animal was a winner.

The burnt shell of the barn rose up out of the green plain, and Rachel slowed Oiche first to a canter, then a walk, ghostly images of her nightmare returning to send a shiver down her spine.

Why would anyone want to burn an old barn which was quite a distance from the house? Was it nothing more than vandalism? She walked Oiche closer to the burnt timbers, but the horse whickered nervously. Rachel soothed it; she knew it disliked the smell of smoke.

She was turning away when she spotted the bright flash of red amongst the timbers. The sudden movement vanished as she turned back.

"Who's there?" she called.

There was no reply, but she distinctly heard the snap of a piece of wood.

Rachel urged Oiche forward, her eyes scanning the ruins, looking for any glimpse of the red. The horse danced sideways, reluctant to approach too close to blackened timbers. Her heart began thumping in her chest. Wood cracked again and she turned to the right – just as a young man darted out of the ruins. Rachel caught a glimpse of bright red hair before he disappeared into a hollow.

"Stop!"

There was no response. Setting her heels to Oiche's flanks she set off after the fleeing figure. As she came around the building, she spotted the boy racing across the flat plain, arms and legs pounding in unison. He was making for a small wood on a slight rise.

Crouching low over Oiche's head, Rachel urged the beast into a gallop, and slowly began to catch up on the young man. He was wearing a dirty white cotton shirt, old stained jeans, battered sneakers and no socks.

Oiche drew closer to the boy. "Stop running," Rachel shouted. "Why are you running?"

The boy ignored her, but she could hear his breath coming in great heaving gasps. Another half dozen strides brought her level with him.

And then the boy turned and shouted at the horse.

The sound was terrifying – a cross between a cat's scream and a dog's snarl. Oiche reared, dancing on her hind legs, forelegs pawing the air. The reins burnt through Rachel's hands as she stood in the stirrups and attempted to stay in the saddle. It took her several heart-stopping seconds before she finally managed to get the horse under control. She knew if she was tossed then the horse could easily trample on her.

When Oiche had stopped prancing, she slid off the horse ... and almost crumpled to the ground. The muscles in her legs, where she had clamped Oiche's sides tightly, were rubbery. Leaning up against Oiche's flanks she could feel the horse's great heart thundering in its body. Its sleek flesh was covered in a fine sheen of sweat and when she attempted to stroke its head, the horse twisted its neck and snapped at her, teeth clicking together inches from her fingers.

The animal was terrified, she realised with a start.

She turned to look for the boy, but he had vanished. She remembered the look on his face though, lips drawn back from his teeth in a terrifying savage grimace, strands of white spittle drooling on his chin. In that instant he had looked like a wild animal ... or a rabid dog.

Suddenly chilled, Rachel pulled herself up into the saddle. She rode back to Seasonstown House without looking back, but she couldn't shake the impression that she was being watched.

4

SITTING ON A CANE CHAIR IN HER BEDROOM before one of the long windows, looking down over the stables, Rachel tried to make sense of her encounter with the red-haired boy.

She had been about to tell her parents, but decided that she'd little enough to tell. What was she going to say: that she'd spotted a boy in the ruins of the barn and then chased him on her horse, and that the boy had shouted and upset the horse? That was all there was to it. And when she looked at it that way, it did seem just a little ridiculous. For all she knew, in the nearest village or town the boy was probably telling his family or friends about the mad girl who had tried to run him down on an enormous black horse. She smiled quickly. How would she have felt if she'd looked over her shoulder and found a horse with its great slab-like teeth virtually nipping at her ear? She'd have screamed too.

But why had he run in the first place?

And why had Oiche been so terrified? On the long ride back to the house, she had felt its heart thundering beneath her legs; she had almost been afraid that its heart would burst.

Maybe it was just highly-strung, a lot of race horses were. But she knew horses, she knew that only something very powerful – very strange – could have frightened it like that.

Maybe if her parents had been at home when she returned, she would have told them, but they had gone up to Dublin to sort out some details with the solicitors, leaving her alone with the servants in the house. She'd eaten a simple salad lunch before taking a shower and changing. She thought briefly about going out again, but the afternoon had turned cool, and she decided to remain indoors and catch up on some mail.

She had promised to write to Kirsty, her best friend, every day, but so far she hadn't managed to find the time to write even one decent letter. Oh, she'd sent a load of postcards, but that wasn't the same thing.

She spent the next hour bringing Kirsty up to date on everything that had happened so far. She stopped writing when she reached the point at which she'd seen the boy, realising that there was something about him, something strange, something which nagged at her. She chewed on the end of her pen. His clothes maybe? His clothes were threadbare and dirty, as if he'd been sleeping rough. He'd been wearing sneakers, she remembered, battered and torn sneakers. His skin was pale, streaked with dirt and ...

His hair!

That was it. His hair. The boy's hair was a bright vivid red ... exactly the same colour as the girl she'd seen working in the stables.

Rachel straightened in the chair. Red hair was not uncommon in Ireland, though in the States that fiery red colour was very rare. She closed her eyes, resting her head against the back of the chair, trying to visualise the red-haired girl ... what was she called again? Maeve, yes, that was it, Maeve.

When she opened her eyes and looked down into the stable yard, she was startled to discover the red-haired girl staring up at her. The girl continued looking even though she knew she'd been seen. This time Rachel returned her gaze, forcing herself to stare at Maeve's hard-boned face. She could see a strong resemblance to the boy, a high forehead, pronounced cheekbones, slightly prominent front teeth. Then slowly, almost deliberately, the girl turned away and crossed the yard, disappearing around a corner.

Rachel took a deep shuddering breath and sat back. She

hadn't realised she'd been holding her breath. The intensity of the girl's gaze had been frightening. She had actually felt the anger in the jade-green eyes staring at her.

She tried to return to her letter, but found that she couldn't concentrate: all she saw when she looked down at the paper were two cold green eyes. She was folding away the page, promising to finish it later, when there was a tentative knock on the door. She jumped.

"Come in," she called, annoyed to find that her heart was racing.

The door opened and one of the staff poked her head in. It took Rachel a few seconds before she recalled the girl's name. "Agnes."

"Yes, Miss," the girl said, obviously pleased that her name had been remembered. She stepped into the bedroom and shut the door behind her. There was a hosepipe coiled around her shoulder. She saw Rachel's surprised look and grinned. "I was told to add water to your bed, Miss. I was going to bring up a kettle, but I thought that would take me all day, so I decided that I'd connect the hosepipe to the tap in the bath and fill it that way."

Rachel stood up and stretched, pressing her hands into the small of her back and arching her spine. Those cane chairs were uncomfortable! "That's a great idea. I felt really queasy and seasick this morning."

"I don't know how you sleep on it," the girl said, uncoiling the pipe on the floor and rolling it into the bathroom. "I prefer my bed solid."

Rachel stripped the eiderdown and sheets off the bed to reveal the black rubbery mattress. She discovered that there were two valves, one on either side.

Agnes came back into the room, brushing strands of her coal-black hair off her forehead with the back of her hand. She

31

knelt beside Rachel and looked at the stoppered valve. "Have you done this before?" she asked.

Rachel shook her head.

"Nor I," the girl admitted, catching the valve and twisting anti-clockwise, following an arrow. "Let's hope there's no accidents," she added grimly.

"Why not?"

"Well, the games room is directly below us. It's got an enormous billiard table in it. I'm not sure your Dad would want a swimming pool as well!" Both girls laughed.

It took several tries and several pints of water squirted across the floor, before they managed to devise a system which allowed Agnes to unscrew the stopper and Rachel to stick in the hosepipe immediately. Then, while Agnes kept the pipe firmly in place, Rachel slipped into the bathroom and turned on the tap, allowing water to trickle through until Agnes shouted stop. When they'd finally finished, the water bed, while still moving and shifting beneath their weight, was a lot firmer.

As Agnes was mopping up the splashes and spillages, Rachel stood out of her way by the window. A flicker of red made her look down. She saw Maeve leading a foal across the yard.

"Who's the red-haired girl in the stables?" she asked suddenly. "About our own age, only bigger."

Agnes's mouth twisted into a sour grimace. "That's Maeve Alton. She's a bit older than us – sixteen or so."

"You don't like her," Rachel said with a smile.

"I've yet to find someone who does. I went to school with her. She has a foul temper and she's as strong as an ox." She laughed quickly. "She's the only girl I know who got into trouble with the head teacher for beating up a boy." Agnes stood up, wiping her hands on a cloth. "Why do you ask?"

"I don't think she likes me," Rachel muttered. "She stares at me with this really fixed expression. It gives me the creeps."

"Oh, she wouldn't cause you any trouble, 'cause your Da owns the place, but she's no time for anyone ... except the horses. She's really good with them, I'll have to give her that."

"Is she from a big family?"

"Her Ma and Da are alive and she has a brother, a year younger than herself. You don't see much of him. He's a bit ... you know ... foolish."

It took Rachel a moment to realise what foolish meant. "You mean he's a slow learner?"

Agnes considered. "Yes, I suppose that's it. He's very shy, keeps to himself, sleeps out in the barns and fields during the summer months. You sometimes see him hanging around the stables. He's got a temper like his sister's though. I suppose all red-heads have a temper. My brother and a few of the local lads were giving him a hard time a couple of months back. One of them tried to push him, but he said it was like pushing a wall."

"What's his name?" Rachel wondered.

"Madoc," Agnes said, "but the lads call him Mad Dog."

Rachel went to bed early. She'd been yawning throughout dinner as she'd listened to her mother and father talk about the difficulty of leasing a particular tract of land they wanted to purchase. She'd excused herself after the meal and headed up to her room, blaming the fresh country air and all the travelling they'd done over the past week for her exhaustion. Before coming to Ireland, they'd first flown to Rome, then onto Berlin and London before finally flying to Dublin.

Too tired even for a shower, she pulled on her pyjamas and – carefully – climbed into bed. It gave slightly beneath her weight and seemed to fold in around her, cradling her. She glanced at the alarm clock – ten o'clock – and smiled. Back home the night would be only starting.

She awoke suddenly, fragments of her dreams flickering around the room, the terrors already disappearing. It was something about a boy whose head had been burning with bright red flames, a horse rearing up before her, hooves flashing, but the horse had the boy's head.

Rachel remained unmoving, eyes wide, staring upwards, desperately trying to work out where she was. Her heart was beating solidly and she was coated in a cold sweat, her pyjamas sticking to her damp skin.

The memories returned. She was in Seasonstown House, in Ireland.

Rolling over in bed, she tilted her small travelling alarm clock to the flickering red glow from outside and read the time: three twenty-five.

She was rolling back over when she suddenly remembered that when she'd awakened last night, the room had been in pitch darkness …

Sudden terror drove her out of the bed, slipping and falling in the tangled sheets before she managed to scramble to the window. Fire was blazing in the straw piled beside the stables, red and orange flames licking at the stonework. She was opening her mouth to scream when the fire alarm went off.

Wednesday, 28th October

5

RACHEL STOOD IN THE DOORWAY and watched her father argue with Sean Summers. Robert Stone had worked alongside the other staff, pouring water onto the burning straw, beating out the flames with sacks or gently coaxing the terrified horses out of their stalls. Now, he was tired and sooty, stinking of smoke, his blond hair filthy ... and in a foul humour. "Accidents like this do not happen!" he roared. "Two fires in two days: does that look like an accident to you?"

Summers shook his head. Like Stone, he was streaked with smoke and soot, and the elbow of his yellow polo neck jumper was scorched brown.

"The police found no evidence that the last fire was set deliberately ..." he began.

"Evidence!" Robert Stone almost spat the word. "What more evidence do you need?" He strode around the room like a caged beast. Rachel stepped back so she wouldn't be seen. "Another couple of minutes and that fire could have spread to the stables ..."

"Begging your pardon, Sir, but the wall and roofs are concrete. The fire wouldn't have spread."

Robert stopped pacing. He walked right up to Summers and poked him in the chest with a rigid forefinger. "If we hadn't got to the fire when we did, the noise of the flames would have panicked the horses, they would have injured themselves in their stalls. Another few minutes and the smoke would have damaged their lungs. Now, this is the second fire here in two days, and I want to know what you're going to do about it!"

Rachel saw the look of surprise on Summers's round face.

Against his soot-smudged face, his grey eyes seemed enormous. "I'm not sure what more I can do. The yard is secured at night of course, but I'll bring in some extra men for round-the-clock security."

"You do that," Robert snapped. "Now go and get some rest. You're no use to me if you're exhausted."

Sean Summers nodded and turned away. Rachel scurried into the dining room seconds before her father strode in.

Elizabeth was finishing breakfast. She had heard every word. "Don't you think you were a bit hard on him?" she asked.

"No, I don't. He's supposed to be in charge here," Robert said bluntly. "If anything had happened to those horses, the bill would have run to millions. Even if news of the fire leaks out, we stand to lose a lot of business anyway." He dropped tiredly onto a chair and bit savagely into a slice of toast while Elizabeth poured him a cup of tea. "We need to find out who is doing this. And why," he added grimly.

"You sound as if this is part of some deliberate plan," his wife said quietly.

Robert nodded. "I'm sure of it. Remember when we bought the stables in Argentina, and those criminals tried to get us to pay protection money? And again in Australia, when that guy tried to cut off our water supply if we didn't pay him three times what he originally agreed. I'm convinced this is something similar." He drained his tea in one quick swallow. "A few scares like the fire last night and Sunday, just to show us what they can do, and then the demand for money." He swore softly.

"What will you do, Dad?" Rachel asked. "You wouldn't sell up, would you?"

Her father smiled tiredly. "I'm not sure if it's worth the hassle." He spread his hands. "Look at me! I'm too old to be fighting fires in the middle of the night."

"But, Dad, you've always wanted stables in Ireland."

Robert saw the hurt look in his daughter's eyes and reached over to squeeze her fingers. "Don't worry, I'm not going to give up just yet. First, if there is a demand for money, we'll agree to pay it, then let the police nab them. Anyway," he continued, "I want you both to be careful. Don't stray too far from the house and keep your eyes open for anything suspicious." He lowered his voice, glancing over his shoulder to make sure none of the servants was around. "And keep your eye on the staff. I wouldn't be at all surprised to find that one of them was in league with these villains."

"If you're so sure it's an extortion racket," Elizabeth said, "why haven't you told the police?"

"Oh, I have," Robert snapped. "I've just been on the phone to them. Some local inspector suggested that it was probably nothing more than vandals!"

Rachel abruptly thought of the red-haired boy she'd seen in the burnt-out barn. She was about to mention it to her parents, but decided to say nothing. There was no point in unduly alarming them and besides, they might stop her from riding.

By the time the police arrived and investigated the cause of the fire – the inspection seemed to consist of nothing more than poking at the smouldering remains with a long stick – it was well into the afternoon. Rachel helped Summers and two stable boys clear away the burnt straw, separating it from the straw at the back of the pile, closest to the stables, which had remained virtually untouched by the fire. She was surprised to discover that there was no sign of the red-haired girl.

It was evening by the time they'd finished, and although she'd planned to go riding, she decided that a bath was more important. She stank of smoke and burnt hay and there were bits of straw everywhere: in her hair, her boots, up her sleeves, down her back. She was sure she was scratched all over.

She was sitting on a chair in her bedroom when her mother poked her head around the door. "Dinner will be ready in a few moments."

"I think I'll give it a miss, Mom. I don't feel so good, and I've got a pounding headache."

"It's the smell of smoke and burnt straw," Elizabeth said quickly, "I'll get you something for it." She left the room and returned a few moments later with a glass of water and two aspirin. "Here, take these. Have a bath; that will help relax you too."

Rachel swallowed the small white tablets. "Thanks, Mom."

"This hasn't been much of a holiday for you, has it?" Elizabeth Stone asked, her eyes crinkling in concern.

Rachel attempted a laugh. "It's certainly different. It beats sitting on a beach."

"We'll make it up to you at Christmas. Your father wants to spend Christmas in Hawaii." She leaned forward and ran her fingers through her daughter's hair, plucking out a handful of twigs. "Have a bath and lie down; you'll feel better."

"I will."

When her mother had left the room, Rachel pulled off her boots and socks and padded barefoot into the bathroom. She turned on the hot taps ... but the water was cold.

"Brilliant," she whispered.

She wandered back into the bedroom and sat down on the edge of the water-bed. She was exhausted; too much excitement and not enough sleep. She lay back on the bed, groaning as the shuddering mattress threatened to unsettle her stomach. She'd heard one of the stable boys say that he was wrecked as they'd finished work. She hadn't understood the phrase then, but she knew exactly what it meant now.

She awoke with a start two hours later.

Rachel groaned and sat up, then held her head until the room stopped spinning around her. She squinted at the clock: it was nearly nine o'clock. She came slowly to her feet; her stomach still felt a little queasy, but her headache had vanished. She stepped into the bathroom and tested the water in the hot tap; it came out scalding. Turning the hot and cold taps on full, allowing the water to thunder into the bronze-coloured tub, she emptied half a bottle of herbal bubble bath into the water. The sharp fragrance of lavender and spices filled the air. On impulse, she added the other half. Pulling off her smoke-stained and bitter-smelling clothes, dropping them into the laundry basket, she wrapped a towel around herself and sat before the sink, cleansing her skin with pads of cotton wool and a milk-white liquid. The cotton balls came away black with soot and grease. She stared hard at her reflection in the mirror. She looked tired, and there were shadows forming under her eyes. Her mother was right; this wasn't turning out to be much of a holiday. At this rate she was going to need another holiday just to recover from this one.

The sound of trickling water startled her. She turned around and saw that the bath had filled and green-tinged bubbles were now frothing over the side.

"Perfect," she whispered. "The perfect end to a perfect day." She was surprised to find herself near to tears.

Turning off the tap, she scalded her arm as she reached down to find the plug and drain off some of the water. She then added some cold water, testing the temperature until she had it just right. When she was finally satisfied, she pulled off the towel and slipped into the deliciously warm, sweet-smelling water. Closing her eyes, she lay back, relaxing her taut, strained muscles. Water trickled over the sides to puddle on the floor. A flickering image of her nightmare – a heaving ship's deck, water splashing in over the sides – returned to haunt her, but she deliberately pushed the thought away, concentrating on more pleasant thoughts.

She wondered what it would be like to spend Christmas in Hawaii.

As the sun sank into the west, it threw the stables into shadow. The figure made its way across the yard, moving swiftly and silently. Horses whickered nervously as it passed their stables, some kicking out fearfully.

It paused at the place where the straw had burnt, raised its head and counted the windows of the house, until it had fixed upon the position of the girl's room. There was no light showing and, since it was far too early for the girl to be abed, that meant that the room was unoccupied.

The shape darted through the shadows, sometimes dropping to all fours, scurrying like a great beast before it reached the wall. Then, using hand-holds and foot-holds that were almost invisible, it smoothly climbed the wall.

Because the day had been hot and close, the window was open.

A floorboard creaked.

Rachel's eyes snapped open.

The board creaked again. That irritating board beside her bed that groaned like an old man's bones every time she pressed down on it. Rachel sat up in the bath, suds cascading from her shoulders.

"Agnes, is that you?"

It wasn't Agnes. It was late now, the bathroom windows dark and blue with night. Agnes would have gone home. Her heart began to thump. Pulling her damp hair off her forehead, she tilted her head to one side, listening. "Mom?"

There was no reply.

Maybe she'd imagined it, or maybe the noise had come from somewhere else in the house ... these old houses were always creaking and groaning. That was it. She smiled at her own nervousness.

She was slowly sinking back into the warm water, when the floorboard creaked again, bringing her up out of the water, heart thundering. There *was* someone outside! They had been standing on the loose floorboard all this time, waiting, listening.

"Who ... who's there?" Her voice was little more than a whisper. She swallowed hard and tried again. "Who's there?"

In the room outside, something crackled like a length of paper tearing. There was a great gasping sigh.

The sound shocked her motionless. She sat perfectly still, staring at the unlocked bathroom door, knowing that the handle would slowly turn and the door would open and ... and ... and ...

Her heart was thumping so hard that the water was trembling in time with it. The water grew chill and the bubbles dissolved into an oily scum on the surface, but still she didn't move, terrified of making any noise.

When she began to shiver uncontrollably, she realised she couldn't stay in the bath any longer. Moving as quietly as possible, she stood up, snatching a towel off the rail to wrap around herself. She look around the room, catching a glimpse of her reflection in the mirror over the bath: she was deathly pale beneath her permanent tan.

She snatched up a can of hairspray and held it before her in both hands, her thumbs on the button. Standing up against the door, she pressed her ear against the cool, damp wood.

She could only hear her thumping heartbeat.

Gripping the handle tightly, she took a deep breath, held it – and jerked the door open!

The bedroom was empty.

She stepped out into the room ... and ice-cold water squelched in the sodden carpet, making her gasp. She rushed across the room, blindly reached for the light, her eyes darting from shadow to shadow, half-expecting them to come alive with sudden movement. She touched the light switch, snapped it on, and turned around ...

Icy terror uncoiled in the pit of her chest, squeezing the air from her lungs. The can of hairspray dropped from suddenly numb fingers.

The water-bed had been ripped apart. A razor-sharp blade had slashed four parallel lines along the length of the mattress, reducing it to a deflated bag, flooding the room with its water.

The door creaked, the handle turned and then burst open – and Rachel screamed before she recognised her father and mother.

6

RACHEL SAT WRAPPED IN HER THICK DRESSING GOWN, with a fluffy towel around her head, while upstairs her father stamped around with Inspector Lanigan. She could hear their voices vibrating through the floor.

Elizabeth Stone was telling her daughter how they had first realised that something was wrong upstairs. "Your father had decided to teach me to play billiards after dinner." She smiled quickly, showing perfect white teeth. "He was getting a bit annoyed because I kept knocking in the balls and he kept missing. Anyway, he was lining up a shot when a drop of water spattered onto the green baize right in front of him. Then another drop splashed onto the balls, and finally a steady stream of water began to drip out of the light fitting." She laughed uneasily. "He was livid; he thought you'd been messing with the bed and released one of the valves."

Rachel looked at her mother. "Who cut the bed, Mom? Why?"

Elizabeth Stone looked from the ruined ceiling to the sodden snooker table. "I don't know," she whispered. "Truly, I don't."

Inspector Lanigan was a tall, broad man in his early fifties, who had played rugby for Ireland in his youth and exercised daily to keep his figure. His hair had once been red but it was now sprinkled with silver and grey and it was hard to find any of its original colour, except at the locks, which were still russet. His cheeks and nose bore a scattering of broken veins. He came from a family of police officers, and he followed a simple rule of policework that had been passed down through the family: look for the simple solution, the obvious answer. Incredibly complex motives and intricate puzzles were usually only found in novels.

"And you say your daughter was the only person in the room, Mr Stone?" he said slowly.

"Yes."

The inspector nodded. He crouched down to examine the four parallel cuts. The cuts themselves were ragged – they were tears rather than cuts – but the material was a thick rubber, and extremely tough. Whatever had made these cuts had been razor-sharp. He'd initially thought about a scissors, but the only scissors he'd managed to find in the room was a small blunt-ended nail scissors. The inspector spaced out the cuts with his short stubby fingers curled into a claw. They fitted almost perfectly. It looked as if someone had dug their nails into the rubber and then dragged their hands the length of the bed ... but that would have taken incredible strength.

Look for the obvious answer.

Standing up, he dusted off his hands. "Would your daughter have any reason to do this, Mr Stone?" he asked.

Robert Stone looked at him in amazement. "Absolutely not!"

"Maybe she resented coming to Ireland," the inspector continued, as if he hadn't heard the answer. "Maybe you and she had an argument and she was upset? Young women often do these things when they're upset ..." he added.

"My daughter didn't do this, Inspector," Stone said icily.

"Perhaps she sees this as a way of catching your attention? A busy man like yourself wouldn't have much time left over for the family, eh, Mr Stone?"

"Spare me your cheap psychology," Stone snapped. "In case it has escaped your notice, this bed is made from rubber,

45

an eighth of an inch thick, sewn in stiffened sections. The slash marks run right across the stiffening. Not only would you need a razor-sharp blade, but you'd also need incredible strength to carry the slashes along for nearly six feet." He pointed to the open window. "Whoever did this came in through the window – my daughter did hear someone in the room after all – they did this for some reason, and then left by the window."

As the inspector was crossing to the window, he asked casually, "And why do you think someone would go to all that trouble to attack a bed?"

Robert took a deep breath before replying. When he finally spoke, his voice was soft, almost gentle. "You can either take this case seriously, Inspector Lanigan, or I can take it to someone who will."

"Oh, I'm taking you seriously," the inspector said, leaning out the window and judging the distance to the ground. "But consider the facts. It's a twenty-foot drop to the ground, with no drainpipe, ivy or footholds visible. When you and your wife came running out of the games room, you had the stairs and the door to your daughter's room in view at all times, and you saw no-one leaving it. You told me you searched the room yourself and found no evidence that anything had been disturbed." He turned around and leaned back against the windowframe. "So what are we left with?" he asked. "I won't insult your intelligence, Mr Stone. Perhaps you should speak to your daughter."

"Inspector, three nights ago a barn on this estate was torched; last night a fire was set in the stables below. That's the fourth fire in a month. Tonight, this house was broken into and my daughter was intimidated. The events are not unconnected. I insist you investigate."

"You insist?" Inspector Lanigan said very quietly.

"I insist."

46

The inspector pushed away from the window, brushing off his hands. "Well, Mr Stone, I would not presume to tell you how to breed horses, and I hope you would not attempt to tell me how to do my job." He nodded at the open window. "Interesting too that the fire below should have started in sight of your daughter's room. We'll be in touch," he said, walking from the room.

"Well?" Elizabeth demanded, a few moments later when Robert came into the games room. He stopped to look at the stained ceiling and the ruined table. "What did he say?" she asked.

"He suggested I talk to Rachel."

"Me?"

"He implied that you slashed the bed. And might have been responsible for starting the fire in the stables last night." Robert raised both hands and shook his head before his daughter could even protest. "Don't worry. I know, I know." He brushed strands of hair off his daughter's forehead and kissed it gently. "Whoever slashed the bed was a lot stronger than you, sweetheart. The inspector is looking for easy answers. Well, don't worry. I've got some very good contacts in this country; the police commissioner is an old friend. I'll give him a ring and explain the situation."

"But why, Dad? Why would someone do something so ... so senseless?"

"Blackmail," Robert said simply. "The fires and the attack on the bed were just a way of showing us how vulnerable we are. Whoever these people are, they're proving that they can get into the stables, or even into the house if they want to. The next step will be to demand money to leave us alone."

Rachel started to shiver violently. She had just realised that someone had been standing in her bedroom with a sharp knife.

What would have happened if she had stepped out into the bedroom ... what would have happened if they had come into the bathroom?

Robert knelt and put his arms around his daughter, squeezing tightly.

"Dad, I'm scared," Rachel whispered.

Robert kissed his daughter's forehead, tasting lavender soap from her skin. But he had nothing to say to her; he didn't want to tell her that he was frightened too.

Inspector Lanigan sat beside the young patrol officer in the white police car, a notebook in his lap. He had twisted around in his seat to look at the house as it slowly receded, only turning away when it finally vanished.

He didn't like Mr Stone, he decided. He was wealthy and arrogant, impatient and clearly scornful of the inspector's efforts. But what he especially disliked was the fact that Stone had threatened to go over his head. Whatever respect Lanigan might have had for the American died right then. He certainly wasn't taking any nonsense from a newcomer who thought he could waltz into the country and start throwing his weight around.

The big inspector looked down at the notebook in his lap and drew a line beneath Rachel Stone's name. He was convinced the daughter was the culprit.

Oh, the Sunday night fire was genuine enough. He had an eye on one or two lads in the nearby towns who might be crazy enough to do that after they'd a few drinks in them. If they'd done it he'd find out soon enough, because they wouldn't be able to keep it quiet. They were sure to boast about it.

The second fire though, the small fire. The girl – Rachel – had probably started that. She could watch it burn from her window ... and hadn't her father said she'd been the first to raise the alarm?

Yes, definitely the girl.

She'd also sliced up the bed. It was a fairly dramatic gesture and guaranteed to catch the father's attention, especially when he'd begin thinking how close his daughter had been to a knife-wielding maniac.

The inspector glanced sidelong at the driver. "You've got children, Mark, haven't you?"

"Yes, Sir. One of each," the younger man said, surprised by the sudden question.

"Just wait until they become teenagers – they'll break your heart." He jerked his thumb back at the house. "This one here has got her Da twisted around her little finger. She's our culprit."

"You sure, Sir?"

"Absolutely."

The bushes parted, and cold green eyes watched the police car disappear into the distance. Then the figure turned and looked back at the house, nostrils flaring as it read the wind, gauging the time.

It would wait until the house was in darkness, then it would return.

7

SITTING ON A DUSTY WINDOW LEDGE, hugging her knees close to her chest, Rachel stared down over the stables. Arc lamps had been fitted at either end of the long line of stables, painting the night in brilliant white light. She could occasionally see figures moving through the pools of light, one of whom she recognised as Summers. She wasn't sure, but she thought he was carrying a shot-gun.

She had been moved to another bedroom, almost directly above her old room. It was small, and rather sparsely furnished, and the bed creaked alarmingly when she sat on it. She had tried lying down and sleeping, but she couldn't bear to close her eyes. She kept hearing the floorboards creaking, then the ripping sound of leather tearing. She knew if she closed her eyes, she would dream of slashing knives.

She wanted to go home. Tears stung her eyes. She had never felt so frightened – so vulnerable – in her life. She'd even bolted the door from the inside, and although the October night was unusually warm and close, she'd made sure that the window was firmly closed.

Her father had tried to explain what was going on: extortion, he called it. First the threats, then the demand for money. She shivered suddenly; the way her Dad had been talking this was only the beginning. Whoever these people were – and she was sure that the red-haired boy and his sister were part of it – they were going to continue. They would keep coming back again and again, until eventually her father paid up. And if he didn't?

What would happen then?

Rachel was climbing off the window ledge when one of the arc lights below went out. She froze, blinking furiously to clear the after-images of light that still burned on her retina. Raised voices echoed flatly on the night air. She tried to make out what they were saying, but they were muffled by the glass. She eased open the window, head turned to one side, listening. Summers was shouting instructions.

There was a muffled explosion of glass, and the second arc lamp died. A wisp of white smoke curled up from the broken light.

There was a deathly silence ... and then glass splintered close by, immediately followed by the rolling boom of a shot-gun exploding across the night.

She threw herself away from the window and scrambled across the floor on hands and knees. She heard the sound of breaking glass again, closer this time. She looked up ... and the bedroom window exploded above her head, showering shards of glass across the floor. Something solid clumped onto the floor by her foot.

Glass shattered in the rooms below her. Again. And again. Cowering behind the bed, she counted four ... five ... six. The shot-gun fired again.

Then silence.

She sat up only when cramped muscles began to twinge. Her foot nudged the object that had come in through the window, moving it on the wooden floor. Without thinking, she leaned forward and picked it up.

It was a brick.

Robert Stone snatched the plastic-bagged brick from Inspector Lanigan's hand and waved it in front of his face. "I suppose you're going to tell me my daughter threw these through the windows?"

51

Robert, Elizabeth, Rachel Stone, along with Sean Summers were gathered in the kitchen with the police inspector and a constable. It was one of the few rooms that wasn't littered with shards of broken glass.

The big inspector looked at the pile of bricks and stones on the kitchen table, then carefully plucked the brick from Stone's hand and returned it to the pile. Seven windows in the east wing had been broken as well as the two arc lights. Some of the windows had been struck with two or three bricks, and the marble fireplace in the drawing room had a deep scar on its glass-like surface where a chunk of rock had bounced off it.

"Someone could have been killed, Inspector."

"I am aware of that," the police inspector said slowly. He picked up one of the bricks and handed it to Robert Stone. "How far could you throw that?"

Robert weighed the brick in his hand. "Not far," he admitted.

The inspector nodded again. "Whoever threw these was close to the house – very close."

Summers pushed himself away from the cooker. "Impossible. Billy and I were patrolling the stables. No-one could have got past us."

What passed for a smile crossed the inspector's broad face. "One brick went through Miss Rachel's window. That's on the third floor, at least thirty-five feet off the ground. Even for someone standing very close to the window, it would be a difficult shot. If you missed, the brick would probably fall back and brain you. Now there's no way someone outside the stable area would have been able to heave a brick that far."

"Not unless they were very strong," Rachel said quietly.

The inspector ignored the interruption. "You fired twice, Sean, what were you shooting at?"

"When the first arc light exploded, we thought it was just

the bulb. Then the second light went. I heard glass breaking in the house at the same time as I caught a glimpse of movement out of the corner of my eye. I fired instinctively."

"Did you hit anything?" Lanigan demanded.

"We'll be having rabbit stew for supper," Summers said with a grin.

"You fired twice," the inspector repeated. "What about the second shot?"

"I thought I saw someone." He ran his hands across his bald head, wiping off droplets of sweat. "I fired without thinking. It was probably just my imagination though."

"You realise you'd be in serious trouble if you'd killed someone, Sean," Lanigan said grimly. "I'd be obliged if you surrendered the weapon at the local station until this mess is cleared up."

"He was defending my property," Robert snapped.

"The law allows for reasonable force, Mr Stone. I don't think a double-barrelled shot-gun could be classified as reasonable force."

"What about a brick through the window, Inspector? What is that classified as?" Stone demanded.

"The shot-gun's legally held, Inspector," Summers said quickly. "I don't see any reason to surrender it."

"If you shoot and wound someone with it, the charge will be attempted murder. If you kill someone, that charge will be murder. Think about that before you use it so freely next time."

"Next time, Inspector?" Stone said icily. "There's not going to be a next time, is there? I want police protection for me and my family."

The inspector didn't reply immediately. He looked at the pile of bricks on the table, each one in a carefully tagged plastic bag. They would have to be sent up to Dublin for forensic examination, though he doubted that they'd find anything. "I think what we have here," he said eventually, "is a simple case of vandalism. It's unfortunate of course, what with you being visitors to this country, but I'm sure it goes on even in your own country. I could certainly give you police protection," he continued, raising his hand for silence, "if any of your lives had been threatened. But that hasn't happened."

"So you're going to do nothing!" Elizabeth snapped.

"I'm sure whoever it was got a good fright when Sean loosed off both barrels at them. I doubt they'll be back." He glanced over his shoulder at the young constable and nodded at the bricks on the table. The man came forward and began loading them into a thick satchel. "Naturally, we'll keep an eye on the local hospital and we'll contact all the local doctors just in case they've treated anyone with a couple of shot-gun pellets in them." He stretched out his hand towards Robert Stone, but the American refused to accept it, and the inspector was forced to lower it, colour flooding his cheeks. "It's late now. I'll send one of my men around in the morning to collect some statements. I'll wish you all a good night."

"And that's it?" Robert Stone asked in astonishment. "You're not going to do anything else?"

The inspector paused at the door. "What else can I do, Mr Stone? Someone threw stones at your window, local lads with a few drinks in them probably. I'll put the word around. I'll see can I find out anything. I'll try and make sure that it doesn't happen again," he added, stepping out into the kitchen yard and pulling the door closed behind him.

Rachel wrapped her arms tightly around her body. She was beginning to realise that this was more than just a simple case of vandalism. This was much more serious, and far more deadly.

Thursday, 29th October

8

SHE WAS LYING IN THE BATH. The water had frozen solid, and a thick crust of ice now held her body trapped beneath the surface, leaving only her head free. She was staring at the door, watching it vibrate in its frame with the force of the blows as someone standing in the bedroom struck it again and again. The wood split – and the gleaming blade of a knife stuck through. Another savage blow hacked off a long splinter of wood and the knife appeared again and again and again.

She pounded frantically at the imprisoning ice with her fists. It cracked in long jagged lines, then abruptly shattered in thousands of shards of sharp glass. She was lying in a bath of broken glass.

Rachel jerked awake with a tiny cry, the nightmare dissolving in the bright morning sunshine. Only the thumping sounds remained. It took her a few moments to realise that the sounds of hammering were coming from the rooms below.

With a shuddering sigh, she lay back in the bed, blinking at the speckling of light across the ceiling as the events of the previous night slid back into place.

Another bedroom.

She had spent three night in this house and had slept in three different beds. This room was next door to her parents'. It was small and smelt stale with disuse, the air thick with whirling dust motes. She was sleeping on a narrow uncomfortable camp bed which Summers had brought in from the stables and carried up to the room. It smelt of straw and horses. "We use it if we have to stay up all night with the horses," he explained, "if one of the mares is about to foal, for example. I know you won't mind the smell." She had been so tired then, she would gladly have slept on the ground.

Rachel sat up carefully, feeling the bed shift beneath her. A musty odour wafted up. She brought her sleeve to her nose and sniffed, wrinkling her nose at the smell of damp straw, old urine and sour sweat. A few hours ago the smell had been fresh and earthy, comforting too, as she had drifted off to sleep. She pulled strands of her hair around in front of her face and breathed in the odour. It too smelt bitter with stale horse-sweat.

Rolling out of the low bed, Rachel grabbed her small bag of toiletries and padded down the hall to the bathroom. The sounds of hammering were louder now and she leaned over the banisters to look down into the hallway. She could see two workmen in the dining room, removing the remains of the shattered window, hammering out the broken glass. Agnes worked behind them, sweeping up the splinters of glass.

Rachel continued down the landing into the bathroom. The room had been decorated entirely in white, white tiles, white porcelain toilet and white sink. It looked, and felt, cold. She was surprised to find that there was no bath, but a shower stall had been fitted in one corner. Leaning on the sink, she stared at herself in a mirrored cabinet which had been fixed to the wall above it. She was shocked at her reflection. There were deep blueish rings beneath her bloodshot eyes, and her usually clear skin was smeared with dust motes from the small dirty bedroom. The skin on her forehead was red and felt rough, and she knew – just knew – that she was going to develop spots over the next few days. She spun the taps angrily. Nothing happened, but the pipes began clattering and clanking.

While waiting for hot water to come through, she crossed to the window, undid the catches and pushed it open, allowing a little of the fresh morning air into the dry, disinfectant-smelling atmosphere of the small room. Resting her elbows on the window ledge, she leaned out the window and stared across the green fields to a distant line of trees. They looked almost black. For as long as she could remember, she had always wanted to visit Ireland ... now she wanted nothing more than to leave, to return home, where she felt safe. From the moment she had seen the burnt shell of the barn, she had felt intimidated, though if she was asked, she couldn't exactly say why.

She was turning away from the window when she looked down and discovered that the bathroom overlooked the stables, but from a slightly different angle than the bedrooms she'd slept in. From here, she could actually see into some of the stables.

A flash of red in the nearest stable caught her attention. The doors were open and she could see the vaguest suggestion of movement in the darkness beyond. She stared into the stable for close to five minutes and was just about to turn away again when two people stepped out into the sunlight.

Her breath caught at the back of her throat.

It was the stable girl, Maeve, and the red-haired boy she'd chased. Now that she saw them together the resemblance was unmistakable. She could tell by the boy's rigid stance and the girl's waving arms that they were having an argument. The girl rounded on the boy and poked him hard in the chest. Rachel saw him stagger back with the force of the blows. The girl suddenly turned and stamped away, leaving the boy standing in front of the stable, his hands dug deep into the pockets of his ragged jeans. He was shaking his head and seemed to be muttering to himself. He pulled his right hand out of his pocket and rubbed at his chest, where Maeve had jabbed him.

Rachel felt a brief pang of sympathy for the boy; the girl

obviously treated him badly. The tap suddenly spat water into the sink in a quick explosion of sound. The boy jerked his head up - and looked straight into Rachel's eyes.

The savage look of loathing on his face sent her scrambling from the window.

"Where's Dad?" Rachel asked, as she stepped into the dining room.

Her mother was just finishing breakfast, a copy of the *Irish Times* spread out before her. "He's gone to Dublin," she said. "He wanted to talk to some friends of his in the government and the police department." Elizabeth looked up from the paper. "How did you sleep?" she asked.

Rachel shrugged. "I'm still tired," she muttered, "and I ache everywhere." She sat down at the table, thought briefly about cornflakes, but finally settled on some dry toast and tea.

Elizabeth Stone folded away the newspaper and dropped it on the floor beside her chair. "Your father wants us to leave until all this trouble is over," she said quietly.

Rachel bit into her toast and said nothing. She felt a huge sense of relief, as if a weight had been lifted off her shoulders.

"He's afraid the situation might become more serious," Elizabeth continued. "He spoke to a police officer in Dublin this morning. They very reluctantly agreed that it might be an attempt at extortion. They added that it might be a paramilitary organisation who would want the cash to buy arms. And they're far more dangerous than ordinary villains."

"What are you going to do, Mom?"

"I'm not going to leave your father alone," Elizabeth said simply.

"Will Dad leave?"

Elizabeth laughed. "I think he'd walk away from the place tomorrow if he could. But he's got this stubborn streak in him, you know that, and it upsets him to think that he's being forced off his own property."

"When are we leaving?"

"As soon as your father makes the necessary arrangements. There are a few contracts which need either to be signed or cancelled. However, you could always leave today or tomorrow."

Rachel drank the lukewarm tea. "I don't want to leave without you," she said quietly. "Dad always said we should stick together."

Elizabeth reached over and squeezed her daughter's hand. "I know that. But this is a dangerous situation. These are dangerous people."

Rachel put down the cup. "But why haven't they got in touch, Mom? What's the point in terrorising us, if they don't demand money?"

"I asked your father the same question. He says we're just being softened up. He's confident that we'll get the demand today or tomorrow."

The sudden tension in her mother's fingers alerted Rachel to the fact that something was wrong. "You're expecting something else to happen, aren't you?"

Elizabeth's grip tightened almost painfully on Rachel's fingers. "All we're doing now is waiting for them to come again. And God knows what they'll do this time."

The constant hammering drove Rachel out of the house. She drifted down to the stables, enjoying the smells and sounds of the horses. Summers tipped his hat as he walked past. "Don't stray too far, Miss," he said.

"I won't."

She was walking past Oiche's stable when the door opened and the stable girl, Maeve, appeared. There was a bucket over her arm and she was carrying a stiff-bristled brush. Her hair and clothes were peppered with wisps of straw.

Before she realised what she was saying, Rachel turned to the girl. "Maeve. Can I have a word with you ...?"

The girl walked past her.

Stung by the deliberate snub, Rachel hurried after the girl, caught her by the arm and attempted to spin her around. It was like trying to move a rock. The girl stopped and turned her head to look at Rachel, her bright green eyes glittering.

"I want to talk to you," Rachel snapped, anger making her voice high and shrill.

Maeve looked into the other girl's eyes, and a look of absolute contempt passed over her face.

"Have you got a problem?" Rachel demanded, moving around to stand directly in front of Maeve.

"No problem." The girl's voice was surprisingly deep and husky. "I've got work to do," she said, and walked around Rachel.

Rachel glared at Maeve's back. "I want to speak to your brother!"

The girl stopped suddenly and turned around. She dropped the bucket and brush onto the ground and stepped right up to Rachel, until their faces were only inches apart. "What do you know about my brother?" she demanded, her accent thick and brutal. She smelt of horse manure and damp straw.

"I want to talk to him," Rachel said firmly, trying to disguise the tremble in her voice.

"Well, he doesn't want to talk to you," Maeve snapped, flecks of spittle splashing onto the younger girl's cheek. "Stay away from him."

"Are you threatening me?" Rachel asked in astonishment. Her thoughts were whirling; this couldn't be happening, not here, not now.

"I'm advising you: stay away from my brother."

"I want to speak to him," Rachel persisted.

"My brother won't speak to you!"

"Why not?"

The girl's breath was foul in Rachel's nostrils. "Because he's dumb. He can't talk to anyone!"

Rachel watched the red-haired girl stomp away. She was trembling and there was a sour taste in her mouth. The anger in the girl's eyes had been terrible, and, for a moment, she thought Maeve was going to strike her.

And why had she lied? Why had she said her brother was dumb? Rachel had seen them talking together. What were they hiding?

9

FROM THE CONCEALMENT OF THE LONG GRASS behind the stables, the figure watched the newcomer speaking to the red-haired girl.

Although it couldn't make out what they were saying, it could sense the anger from them, and for a moment it thought that Maeve would strike the blond girl.

But then the moment passed and the red-haired girl stomped away. The other girl remained standing in the same spot for a few moments, breathing deeply, calming herself, then she turned and headed back towards the house.

The figure turned and looked at the house again. It would have to go back in. It would have to teach them the meaning of fear.

RACHEL STUMBLED ACROSS THE LIBRARY almost by accident. It was on the ground floor, but right at the very back of the house, quite close to the kitchens.

She had spent much of the afternoon wandering around the old house, opening doors, discovering a few surprises – a fully fitted nursery, complete with an enormous dolls house, a small narrow room where the walls were completely covered with tiny, beautifully painted portraits and a huge wine cellar. She had actually been coming up from the dusty cobwebbed cellar when she spotted the door, almost lost in the shadow thrown by the stairs.

Entering the room was like stepping back into the past.

Three of the walls were covered in bookshelves, tightly packed with books. Two long windows took up the fourth wall. Ivy-choked bushes grew tall and wild outside the windows, throwing the room into a green-tinged shadow.

Rachel stepped into the library and closed the door behind her, breathing in the dry atmosphere of dust and leather, of polish and decomposing paper. She pressed the light switch and a low wattage bulb flickered on. The girl walked slowly around the room, not touching anything, simply looking at the shelves.

Most of the books were bound in full leather. Rachel had always thought that leather was just one colour, but now she realised that it ranged from a deep, almost black colour, to a light tan. There were white bindings amongst them too – she knew they were vellum – and a few others in a stippled cloth, which she guessed was buckram. Her father had a few fine books back in the apartment in New York, but they were mainly for show and investment, and although he was able to speak with great authority about the books in his small library, about the binding, the paper, and the illustrations, she knew he was only repeating what he'd read in the catalogue. She idly wondered how much the library was worth. Thousands probably, maybe hundreds of thousands.

The room was bare except for a long low table and an ancient leather swivel chair that had seen better days. The leather backing was dry and cracked and the seat had caved in to a deep curve.

Rachel sat in the chair and placed her hands on the table, looking around at the book-filled shelves. It was very easy to imagine one of the previous owners of the house sitting here, in this very chair, looking at the library, perhaps reaching out to pluck a book off the shelves to read through on some dark winter's night.

A sudden thought struck her. She realised that she knew absolutely nothing about the previous owners of Seasonstown House. Oh, she knew the jockey, Tommy Allen, had owned the house, but what about the people who had lived in it before him? She looked at the shelves again: if there was any information about the owners or about the house, surely it was here in this room?

On impulse Rachel swung around in the creaking chair to look at the shelves directly behind the desk, in a narrow bookcase between the two tall windows. At home, the books she used most frequently were on the shelf nearest to her bed. She ran her fingers down the books on the shelves and nodded: these books had obviously seen more use than the others. The leather was stained dark with the grease of countless fingers, and blue ink had speckled the edges of one of the shelves. She plucked a long narrow volume off the shelf and heaved it around to the table. As she slapped it down, dust rose in a fine grey cloud, and she sneezed uncontrollably. When she opened the book, she discovered it was a series of daily accounts, starting in the year 1800. The last date in the book was 1810. All the entries were in a broad flowing spidery handwriting, and almost impossible to read. She stood up and heaved the book back onto the shelf. There were ten years' accounts in the book, and there were at least another twenty books like it piled up on the shelves. She was looking at two hundred years' work!

A series of short fat books next caught her attention and she pulled out the nearest one. It was bound in a dark hard leather. There were four triangular pieces of metal on the corners of the covers and a simple metal catch locked the covers together. When she put the book down on the table, the catch swung loose.

The cover cracked as she opened it, tiny flakes of old leather speckling the table. Rachel carefully turned the brittle yellow paper. A flower had been pressed between the first two pages. Paper-thin and tiny, it was still recognisably a buttercup. Below it was a name and date in neat precise writing: Piers de Courtney, 17th August 1789.

Rachel looked at it in something like awe. Over two hundred years ago, Piers de Courtney had plucked a flower – probably from the lawn outside, and carefully pressed it between these pages. She turned the page, the corners flaking away at her touch, and discovered that the book was a diary, the pages covered in the same precise script. In places the ink had faded to a rusty brown and was almost impossible to read. The first entry was for January 1st, 1789.

"We must give thanks that this first day of the Year of Our Lord, Seventeen Hundred and Eighty Nine, has dawned without the howl-

ing storms that have kept us virtual prisoner here since the Eve of Christmas ..."

Rachel carefully spelled out the words, squinting to make out the writing, but the letters were very faded. She turned to the back of the book, wondering if the writing would be clearer. The last pages were blank. She skipped back through the pages looking for the last entry. She discovered it close to the middle of the book.

"This day, the Thirty-First of October, All-Hallows Eve, the clan of Natalis came."

There was no other entry.

Puzzled, Rachel turned back to the shelves, and pulled down another diary. It was in de Courtney's handwriting, but finished on the 31st of December 1788. The book beside it started in 1786 and finished on the 31st of December 1787. The writing here was not quite so neat, the letters larger, and the book was speckled with ink blots.

Rachel picked up the first book again. What had made a diarist who had kept regular diaries for such a long period, decide to stop? She looked at the last entry again. The writing looked hurried, jagged, the letters biting deeply into the page.

"... the clan of Natalis came."

Natalis didn't sound like an Irish name. Was it French? Italian? But then, de Courtney didn't sound like an Irish name either. Could it be French or Norman? Hadn't Ireland been invaded by the Normans? She shook her head; she knew so little of Irish history.

Rachel had picked up the diary again when the gong

boomed close-by, making her jump. She looked at her wrist-watch, surprised to discover that it was nearly half-past seven. She had spent the afternoon here. She stretched, easing her stiffened neck muscles, and then looked at her hands, which were filthy with the dirt and dust off the old books.

The dinner-gong boomed again. Still clutching the diary, Rachel hurried from the room, realising that she had better wash her hands before she sat down for dinner.

From the concealment of the bushes outside the window, cold green eyes watched the girl leave the library. The figure had been watching her since she had entered the room. It had memorised every detail of the girl: her shimmering golden hair – it had never seen anything so bright – her skin, so soft and clean, her eyes, blue like the early morning sky. When the girl sat at the desk, she was effectively hidden from the garden, and it had taken an enormous effort of will to remain in the bushes, knowing that she was only a few feet away.

The bell startled the figure, and it came alert, ready for flight. The bell had obviously summoned the girl. When it rang again, she hurried from the room, pulling the door shut behind her.

The figure in the bushes waited a few moments longer, then crept out of its hiding place and approached the windows ... .

RACHEL STONE STOOD IN THE DOORWAY and felt her dinner heave in her stomach. She swallowed hard, desperately resisting the urge to vomit.

She had returned to the library after dinner, drawn by curiosity. When she turned the handle, the door opened a couple of inches, then stopped. Surprised, she pushed hard at the door and heard something scrape across the wooden floor.

When she finally managed to push it open wide enough to squeeze through, she discovered that the room had been destroyed.

All the books had been pulled from the shelves and scattered across the floor. Most were in shreds, and wisps of paper still circled in the air. Heavy leather bindings had been torn off and snapped in half, the thick leather shredded, the paper crumbling to dust. The chair she'd been sitting in less than an hour before had been snapped in two and a hole punched through the seat, the leather backing hanging in long dangling strips. Wiry horsehair stuffing poked through the rents. The polished table was scarred by four long streaks slashed across the wood. A broken light-bulb swayed in its socket.

"Mom," Rachel said, but the sound came out in a hoarse whisper. She swallowed hard. "Mom," she tried again. "Mom!" This time it came out in a piercing scream that brought Elizabeth Stone running. At the same time the door from the kitchen burst open and Sean Summers rushed out, a riding crop clutched firmly in his hands.

Elizabeth gathered her daughter into her arms and held her while Summers stepped cautiously into the room, looking around in astonishment. The frenzied destruction shocked him. He picked up a binding that had been snapped in two, and wondered at the great strength it would have taken to do that. When he traced the scars on the wooden table, he felt something cold slide down the back of his neck: the scratches matched the spread of his fingers. He thought of claws and shuddered.

"What happened here, Sean?" Elizabeth Stone asked.

The estate manager shook his head. "I don't know, Ma'am," he admitted. He nodded at the open window. "Someone entered through that window..." he began, then stopped. He ran his fingers down the side of the window frame, feeling the splintered ridges of wood. The lock had been torn off, the metal twisted and buckled, the glass cracked with the force of the blow. Leaning out of the window, he looked at the ground. But the hard, dry earth carried no tracks.

"When is Mr Stone back, Ma'am?" he asked, turning back into the room.

Elizabeth looked at her watch, squinting in the evening gloom. It was close to nine o'clock. "I would have expected him back by now," she said, and immediately felt the first whispering butterflies of fear in the pit of her stomach. "I'll phone him in the car," she said decisively.

Summers nodded. "Should we report this to the police?" he wondered aloud, looking at the room again, shaking his head at the senseless destruction.

"Why bother?" Elizabeth said bitterly. "That inspector is certain Rachel's responsible. He'd be even more convinced if he learned that she discovered this."

Summers lifted a book – Rachel recognised it as one of the accounts books she had looked at earlier. The four-inch thick book had been cleanly broken in half like a piece of wood. "Miss Rachel didn't do this, Ma'am." He attempted to break one of the covers, but succeeded only in bending it slightly. "Even Inspector Lanigan will have to admit that."

"Mr Summers," Elizabeth Stone said quietly, "would you please check the rest of the house, just in case there's an intruder hiding in one of the rooms. I'll phone my husband now. Rachel, you come with me."

Rachel nodded. She took a last look around the ruined library and wondered who or what could have done this amount of damage in such a short space of time. She suddenly looked at the estate manager. "Mr Summers, how long were you in the kitchen?"

He looked surprised. "I don't know how long exactly, Miss. I came in for my dinner around half-seven or so." He nodded. "Must have been around then. 'Coronation Street' was on the TV."

Rachel and Elizabeth looked at him blankly.

Summers smiled sheepishly. "It's a soap opera. It starts at half-seven and finishes at eight."

"Did you hear anything, Mr Summers?" Rachel asked.

Summers started to shake his head then he suddenly realised the point Rachel was making. Elizabeth Stone drew in a sharp breath when she too realised the implications of Rachel's question. Whoever had wrecked the room had done so in complete silence.

Summers returned to the sitting room as Elizabeth Stone slammed down the phone. She had been trying to reach Robert for the past five minutes, but his car phone wasn't responding. A taped message on the line kept repeating: *"The number you require is unavailable. Please try again later."*

"There's no-one in the house, Ma'am."

"I cannot contact my husband. Apparently, he left Dublin about thirty minutes ago, but the car phone is not responding."

Summers glanced at his watch. "He should be here in the next thirty minutes or so. The car's probably in one of those areas where the carphone network doesn't work."

Elizabeth nodded. She turned back to the window and folded her arms across her chest, staring out into the night, looking down the drive, hoping to see the sweep of approaching car headlights.

"I think I'll stay here until he arrives," Summers said, and then added quickly, "if that's all right with you."

"Thank you, Mr Summers, I would appreciate that," Elizabeth Stone said, without turning around. Sean Summers sank into one of the soft leather chairs across from Rachel and resisted the urge to yawn. He was desperately tired. He'd only had about three hours' sleep last night. His eyes felt gritty and there was the suggestion of a headache at the base of his skull. To try and stay awake, he smiled at Rachel. "Are you all right, Miss?"

The girl nodded. Her initial shock at discovering the destruction of the library had turned to a cold anger. It was all so senseless: why destroy something so old on a whim? What did it achieve? She looked across at Summers, noticing the slight sheen of sweat on his bald head. "Who did this, Mr Summers?"

The estate manager looked surprised. "What do you mean?"

"I didn't mean to make it sound like an accusation," she apologised. "I was just wondering if you had any idea who might have done this. The inspector said something about local lads in one of the nearby towns. Why would they do this?"

"I don't know, Miss." Summers shook his head, but Rachel saw the sudden evasive look in his eyes.

"Have the locals any reason to bear us a grudge?" the girl persisted.

Elizabeth Stone turned from the window and looked at Summers.

The young man ran his hand across his bald head in a quick nervous gesture. "I'm sure they haven't, Miss."

Elizabeth went to sit beside her daughter. "What are you not telling us, Mr Summers?" she demanded.

The Irishman looked at the two women. In that instant they looked so alike, their faces set in identical determined expressions, their blue eyes anxious and searching.

"Well?" Elizabeth said softly.

Summers leaned forward in the seat and rested his forearms across his knees. He locked both hands together. Without meeting the women's eyes, he said, "There has been some local opposition to your coming here."

"Why?" Rachel asked. She felt they were very close to something here ... and at the back of her mind, she couldn't help but wonder how Summers, who had been sitting almost next door to the library, had heard nothing. The crack of a leather binding snapping must have sounded like a gunshot. The man obviously knew much more than he was telling, and right now she was beginning to wonder if he wasn't actually involved.

" A lot of locals lost their jobs when Mr Stone purchased this place," Summers said quickly. "The previous owner, Tommy Allen, employed a lot of them as gardeners, handymen, cooks, decorators, stable boys and girls and grooms. All the food and drink for the house was purchased in the local towns, all the vegetables and hay from the local farmers."

Mother and daughter glanced at one another, wondering where this was leading.

"Then Mr Stone bought this place, and the lawyers and accountants moved in and began going over the figures. They discovered that we were employing far too many people and

73

that we could buy the food cheaper in Dublin. Twenty jobs vanished overnight, and over the past couple of months, two of the local shops have been forced to close down because they were no longer supplying the house." He shrugged his shoulders. "So you see why there's little enough love for you in the local towns and villages."

"Do you think that the locals might be getting their own back by attempting to terrorise us – a little revenge for what we did to them?" Elizabeth asked.

"I didn't say that," Summers said quickly. "I was just telling you how the local people feel about you."

"But I think we can put two and two together," Elizabeth Stone said grimly. "And where does the inspector fit into all this?"

A ghost of a smile flitted across Summers's thin lips. "His wife owned one of the shops that closed down."

Elizabeth and Rachel nodded together. Suddenly it began to make a sort of sense. And now that they knew the reason – or at least a probable reason – for the disturbances, they suddenly didn't seem so frightening anymore.

Car headlights flashed across the window. Elizabeth stood up and crossed to the door. "That will be Robert," she said gratefully.

ROBERT STONE TURNED THE BMW into the long drive with a sigh of relief. It had taken him far longer to drive from Dublin than he'd expected and he was exhausted after a day of meetings and briefings, first with his solicitor, then with various accountants, bankers and financial backers. His last meeting of the day had been with the Minister for Justice and the Police Commissioner. They listened politely to his story about the fires, the slashed water-bed and the shattered windows. They were rather sceptical at first, inclined to dismiss his complaints as nothing more than vandalism, which they apologised for, and promised that the local police would take care of it. They obviously expected him to leave then, but Robert Stone had been dealing with politicians for a long time. It took him an hour before he had convinced them that this was no simple case of vandalism, pointing out the similarities with happenings in Australia and South America. But it took the threat of going to the press with the story before the two men had agreed to send a special anti-terrorist unit down to Seasonstown House to investigate.

When Robert Stone left the minister's office, he drove straight into the evening traffic. When he'd left for Dublin earlier that day, Elizabeth had suggested he take one of the staff with him to act as a chauffeur and guide, but he had refused. He had been to Dublin on at least a dozen previous occasions, and always found he could navigate his way easily around the surprisingly small city. But driving through the evening traffic, he discovered that its small and compact size ensured that the traffic jams were quite ferocious. He attempted to phone Seasonstown House on the car phone, but the line was a buzzing crackle caused by the surrounding buildings. Once he left the city behind however, traffic gradually thinned out, until in places he had the road to himself. He relaxed, enjoying driving the powerful car.

The evening drifted into night almost unnoticeably, and it was only when the oncoming cars flashed him with their headlights that Robert realised that he was driving with no lights. He flicked on the lights and thumbed the switch that lowered the windows a fraction, allowing the cool, earth-scented breeze to waft into the car. He immediately felt fresher, more alert. The air tasted fresh and clean, moist with greenery, with just the hint of the oncoming winter in the night air – a sharp nip.

He came to a decision on the long drive back from Dublin: he would send Elizabeth and Rachel away. They could go and spend some time shopping in London or Paris, or head back to the States if they wanted to. It was pointless exposing them to a risk here. And once they were out of the way, it would be one thing less for him to worry about. He'd sort things out here, put a breeding and training programme in place, maybe replace Summers as manager and bring in someone older and more experienced, possibly one of his Australian men, before heading back home for Thanksgiving Day on November 26th.

He had actually driven past the sign for Seasonstown House, before he realised it. He reacted automatically, slamming on the brakes, sending the heavy car into a skid. Dry brown dust clouded up around the car. Realising how stupid he'd been – if anything had been coming behind him, they would probably have driven straight into the back of the car – he put the car into reverse and swivelled around in his seat to look behind him, before slowly driving back to the junction with the minor road. As he turned around again, a flicker of reddish fur moved at the corner of his eye. Fox, maybe?

A few miles down the winding country road, the house loomed up off to his left. From the distance it looked as if every light in the house was on. Robert frowned ... something was wrong. He pressed down on the accelerator, the car lurching forwards, headlights stabbing the gloom. Gravel crunched beneath his wheels as he sped up the long driveway.

A shape stepped out from behind the bushes that lined the road.

He saw the figure an instant before the car struck it. He jammed on the brakes, but too late. There was a solid thump and then a body was tossed up onto the windscreen, spider-webbing the toughened glass. It bounced up onto the roof and slid off along the back window and boot.

The car slewed to a halt in a shower of gravel, jerked and cut out as Stone lifted his foot off the clutch. He sat still for a moment, clutching tightly to the steering wheel, while his heart thundered in his chest. I have just killed someone. The thought ran round and round in his head in a monotonous chant. I have just killed someone!

He flipped open the glove-box and pulled out a short-handled torch. Then, taking a deep breath, he scrambled out of the car and hurried back along the road, the torch light flickering along the gravel, looking for the body.

There was none.

Stone stopped at the spot where he thought the body had landed. Maybe it had bounced into the bushes ... but they seemed undisturbed. Kneeling, he examined the gravel closely. His own tyre marks were clearly outlined where they had bitten right through the covering of stones into the soft soil beneath. A moist spot flickered, shining blackly in the light and he reached down to touch it with trembling fingers.

Blood.

Now that he knew what he was looking for, he was able to see the scattered speckles of blood on the ground. But they didn't seem to go anywhere: they didn't lead into the bushes, or back down the track.

Robert walked back to the car, playing the torch across the bodywork. The front bumper was mangled, there was a deep dent in the bonnet, the windscreen had been bowed in with the force of the blow and there was a hollow in the roof where the body had hit it and, most disturbing of all, a long series of scratches down the back window and boot, as if something had clung on to the car. Nothing could have inflicted that amount of damage and survived, he reasoned: there should have been blood everywhere. He walked slowly back down the track again, looking for evidence that something had crawled into the bushes, playing the torch beam across the leaves and branches. Nothing. No signs of blood, no broken or twisted branches, no crumpled leaves. Whatever he'd hit had vanished.

Robert lifted his fingers and looked at the blood stain again. Without the evidence of the blood and his mangled car, he'd almost have believed he imagined it.

From behind the bushes, cold green eyes watched Robert Stone climb back into the car and drive very slowly up to the house. Only then did the figure come to its feet, whimpering with pain. It didn't think there was anything broken, but there were cuts and bruises everywhere. It grinned, showing its teeth. It wondered how Stone was feeling.

IN THE LONG BARE ROOM, twelve shapes moved in the darkness, congregating in the corner close to the boarded up window. The stale air was rank with the musky odour of old sweat and the sweeter odour of diseased flesh.

In the corner, a figure lay on an old mattress stuffed with straw. "Well?" it wheezed. "Tell me."

"The accidents of the past few days have frightened them. I fear they will leave," a young woman whispered.

"They must not be allowed to leave. I have not lived this long to fail at the last step. You must ensure that they remain here!"

"How?" the young woman asked.

"Give them a reason not to leave."

"What sort of reason?" the young woman wondered.

"Take something precious from them. Something they will not leave without. Do you know anything which they would hold dear?"

The young woman nodded. "I believe I do."

RACHEL COULD HEAR HER PARENTS ARGUING in the bedroom next door. She couldn't make out the words, but she could guess that her father wanted them to go away.

He had been deathly pale when he had arrived home that evening. Without even waiting to hear about the break-in to the library, he immediately sent her to bed. She knew from the look on his face that arguing was a waste of time.

He left the house with Summers and she didn't hear the car start up, so she knew he was somewhere in the grounds. Still fully clothed, she lay down on the bed, with her hands behind her head, dozing lightly. A sharp rapping on the hall door made her instantly alert and she hopped out of bed and crouched by her open bedroom door, listening as her father returned with Summers. They then spent nearly an hour in the sitting room with her mother, but the door was closed and Rachel couldn't make out what they were saying. When the manager finally left, close to midnight, she watched through the banisters as her father carefully locked and bolted the heavy door. She scuttled back into her room and undressed quickly as she heard him moving around the house, locking all the doors and checking the windows. She'd just hopped into bed when he tapped gently on her door and opened it. She sat up, pretending to blink sleep from her eyes. "Is everything all right, Dad?"

"Everything's fine, sweetheart." He stepped into the room, and sat down on the edge of the bed, taking her hand in his. "I heard about the library," he said softly.

Rachel shuddered. "It was creepy, Dad. I keep thinking that

whoever did it was probably standing outside the window, watching me."

Robert Stone shook his head quickly. "I doubt it. They probably saw that the room was empty and simply made the most of the opportunity."

"But why, Dad?" she asked.

Her father shrugged. "To frighten us. Are you frightened?" he asked.

Rachel thought for a moment before answering, then she nodded. "I'm scared, Dad."

He nodded again. "There's a special police unit coming down to investigate tomorrow. That might put a stop to everything."

"Did Mom tell you what Summers told us about the locals losing their jobs and that horrible inspector's wife owning one of the shops that went bust?"

"Your mother made Summers repeat the story to me. It could be vandals trying to frighten us, or locals getting a little revenge, but I doubt it. I'll pass it on to the police tomorrow and we'll see what they say. Anyway," he continued, "I want you and your mother to leave here for a while. Go to Dublin, or better still, go to London or Paris."

Rachel shook her head, and in that instant looked so like her mother than Robert had to smile. "I'm not leaving you here on your own," she said defiantly. Robert Stone leaned forward and kissed his daughter's forehead. "Your mother said exactly the same thing," he said. "We'll talk about it in the morning."

Although the night was cool, Rachel felt hot and sticky; she wondered if she was coming down with a chill. Throwing back the sheets, she swung her legs out of bed. She wanted a glass of water ... but she realised she was reluctant to leave the bedroom. She had even locked the bedroom door, something she only ever did in hotels.

The room was airless. Rachel crossed to the window. It took her a moment to work out that a catch had to be turned in the centre of the window frame, which allowed the bottom half to be lifted up. She pressed her forehead against the cold glass, feeling the delicious trickle of cool air across her hot skin.

Rachel returned to bed, sat up against the pillows, and snapped on the bedside light. She was too alert to sleep. Lifting her watch off the locker, she tilted its face to the light. One-fifteen. She slid down in the bed, resting her hands behind her head. She wanted a cool drink and something to read, but she'd left her magazine in the sitting room, and she wasn't going to venture out into the halls alone. Not at this hour, not after what had happened during the day. And despite what her father had said, she knew that someone had been standing outside the library while she'd been reading the books.

The book!

A sudden thought struck her and she stopped. What had happened to the book she'd taken from the library? Sitting up, she looked around the room. She'd brought it back up here, hadn't she? The book was on the wicker chair behind the door, half buried beneath the clothing she'd piled up on top of it, the dark leather binding blending in with the background.

Hopping out of bed, she swept her clothes onto the floor, picked up the book and then dragged the chair over to the light. She angled the shade so that it shed more light on the ancient book. Her fingers traced the outline of a design that had been cut into the cover which she hadn't noticed before. She could just about make out a shield-like crest, showing a man's face, flanked by two beasts' heads – dogs, lions? There were some words around the edge of the crest, but she couldn't make them out.

Easing apart the catch, Rachel opened the book and came across the pressed buttercup again. She looked at the name and date below it, imagining herself holding a pen to shape the letters.

Piers de Courtney, 17th August 1789.

America had been a young nation when Piers de Courtney had written his name and date. The French Revolution was still in progress, the Bastille had just fallen, Napoleon had not yet come to power. For the first time in her life, she felt a sense of history. This book was a part of history.

Rachel read the first entry again, struggling with the faded letters.

"We must give thanks that this first day of the Year of Our Lord, Seventeen Hundred and Eighty Nine, has dawned without the howling storms that have kept us virtual prisoner here since the Eve of Christmas ..."

She wondered what it would have been like to be stuck for a week in this house – would it have been cold and draughty? – while storms howled around the chimneys. The de Courtneys were obviously wealthy, they would have lived lives of comfort: what about the peasants who lived on their lands – how would they have fared that Christmas week?

"We supped well with our friends and neighbours and made right merry, celebrating the new year in proper fashion. Towards midnight the dogs set up a terrific howling which greatly disturbed the proceedings. Father sent the servants out into the grounds with muskets to investigate. But they returned with the sorrowful news that three of our mastiffs had been slaughtered in a most barbarous fashion.

"What manner of man kills a dumb beast? What is gained by it?

"The death of his favourite hounds disturbed Father greatly. I

offered to ride into the nearby villages and flog a dozen men as an example of what would happen to those who dared do such a thing. But Father refused, saying that the villagers were innocent. When I questioned him further, he replied saying that it was likely the work of the clan of Natalis."

Natalis? Rachel stopped. Where has she heard that name before? She suddenly turned to the the middle of the book, flicking to where she'd discovered the last entry.

"This day, the Thirty-First of October, All-Hallows Eve, the clan of Natalis came."

She turned back to the opening pages of the book.

"Father will say no more, but I am determined to discover the whereabouts of this family, and teach them the lesson they deserve."

Rachel smiled at de Courtney's pompous language. She wondered how old he was. She'd originally thought he was a grown man, but reading the diary, she got the impression that he was not much older than herself. She knew boys like him back in the States: wealthy, pompous, self-important ... and boring.

Who were these Natalis people?

She was turning the thick crumbling page when she heard the noise. Deep in the house something tore. The book slipped from her hands, fell to the floor and split open.

The tearing noise came again, a long ragged broken sound, followed by the sound of cloth being ripped.

Rachel rose slowly to her feet, staring intently at the door. Had she locked it?

Then there was a high-pitched screech, like a nail drawn

down a blackboard, that set her teeth on edge. She distinctly heard glass cracking.

Cloth ripped and tore again, and then a series of rattling thumps confused her ... until she realised it was someone knocking their hands against the banisters.

Which meant they were coming upstairs.

Wood snapped and snapped again, and she heard a stick or large piece of wood falling onto the floor of the hallway. It bounced twice in the silence, then rattled still.

A stair creaked.

Rachel distinctly heard the scratch of fingernails being dragged up the banister rail. There was a crack and what sounded like paper being torn.

Her eyes were now fixed on the thin strip of light that showed beneath her door, where her father had left the landing light on.

Something was torn off the walls to her left – paper? – and then the wall vibrated as it was struck heavily.

It was coming closer.

Closer.

A shadow appeared in the light under her door. And the handle slowly turned.

Her heart was thundering so loudly she couldn't hear anything else. Her breath came in great gulps. But she couldn't find the breath to scream, could only watch as the handle was twisted gently, and then the door rattled as whoever stood on the other side attempted to push it open. When they found it was locked, a solid blow thumped against the wood. Then another, harder this time. And another. There was a crack and a narrow split appeared in the wood.

There was a sudden shout from her parents' room. Surely they hadn't slept through the noise? She could hear her father's voice yelling, swearing, cursing, and then Rachel realised that the intruder was gone from her door.

She heard her parents' bedroom door open, and she suddenly found she could move again. She had been rooted to the spot with fright. She was passing the window, running to the door, when she saw movement in the yard below. A shape scurrying from shadow to shadow. It paused once, turned and looked up at Rachel's lighted window. When it saw her shape silhouetted against the glass, it turned and ran, but not before the girl had caught the glimpse of bright red hair.

Friday, 30th October

15

SOMETHING POWERFUL AND TERRIFYING had moved through the house. Long jagged scratches had been gouged into the walls, and wallpaper and curtains hung in ragged strips. Several of the banisters had been broken in half, and long cuts dug deeply into the polished wood. White scratch marks ran down the huge mirror in the hall. A hole had been punched in an ugly oil landscape beside it, the thick canvas pulled out of the frame. Three parallel ragged cuts ran up the wall to Rachel's room, and the door itself had been split from top to bottom with the incredibly powerful blows.

It was only when she looked at the door that she realised that another blow would have shattered it in two.

The police were all over the house. The three-man anti-terrorist unit had arrived shortly after the local police. Lanigan, the local inspector, once again attempted to dismiss the incident, pointing out that the worst damage had been to Rachel's room. However, Detective Inspector Michael Feeney, in charge of the special unit, took one look around the house and dismissed the inspector, ordering him to begin an immediate inspection of the grounds.

While Robert and Elizabeth were giving their statements to the other officers, the Detective Inspector took Rachel through the house, talking quietly to her, taking the time to gain her confidence, listening to her. He was a big, bulky man with a long narrow, rather sorrowful face.

He began by showing her the broken pane of glass in the kitchen door. "He came in through here. Broke the glass, reached in and turned the key." The big man smiled quickly.

He brushed strands of his thinning black hair off his forehead. "Never leave the key in the lock." He traced three ragged cuts on the wooden kitchen table. "These were done with a sharp instrument, probably one of those little garden forks with three teeth." He pointed to the kitchen door. It too bore three cuts. Opening the door he led the girl down along the hall. The cuts scarred the wall. "He walked down this way, dragging the fork along the wall." He pointed to the scratched mirror and the torn picture. "Our friend stopped here for a moment for a little senseless vandalism, then started up the stairs." He touched the banisters where two of the rods had been knocked out. "He must have kicked these. He then continued up the stairs. Scratched the wall again." Here the scratches were so deep that they had torn out chunks of the plaster beneath the covering of wallpaper. In places, whole sheets of wallpaper hung almost to the floor.

"Why didn't Mom and Dad hear anything?" Rachel asked.

The inspector smiled quickly. "Because it happened so quickly." He swept an arm around. "All of this damage was done in a matter of minutes. Your parents only awoke when this person began pounding on your door."

When they reached the landing, they discovered a small sandy-haired man in white overalls crouched on the floor beneath Rachel's door, carefully tugging at splinters with a long tweezers.

"Anything useful, Tom?" the inspector asked.

The smaller man shook his head. "I'm not sure what he hit the door with. There's no evidence of a blade, so you can discount an axe or something like that. Nor is there any evidence of dirt or footprints on the door, so I don't think he kicked it. Looks like he just punched it." The small man smiled briefly, showing crooked teeth. "And he punched it real hard."

"Like in karate?" Rachel asked. "I used to do karate. I've

watched guys breaking blocks and bricks and lengths of wood."

Feeney looked at the technician. "Could it have been a martial arts blow?"

"Could be; that's a good idea. But whatever it was, it was incredibly powerful." He tapped the door. "This is solid oak."

Feeney then led Rachel back downstairs. "Now, I want you to tell me exactly what you saw and heard. Take your time and leave nothing out, you never know how important it might be." They stepped out into the cool morning air. A watery October sun rode low in the sky and the air was damp and chill with the night's dew still thick on the grass.

"Inspector Lanigan believes I did it," Rachel said quietly.

"Well, just between you and me, Inspector Lanigan's a fool. I've reviewed the evidence, and I don't see how you could be involved. What is clear, though, is that the attacker is concentrating on you. He obviously thinks he can get to your father through you."

"So you do think this is a kidnapping or blackmail attempt?" she asked, relieved. Her father had been right!

"Absolutely. All the signs are there. First they terrorise you, show how easily they can get to you, then they demand money. It's a very neat scheme, because they don't even have to kidnap you and have the bother of looking after you. Now," he continued, "tell me everything."

Lying in the long damp grass on the other side of the field, cold green eyes watched the girl talking to the newcomers. She had been at the window last night. The figure in the grass wondered what she had seen.

Rachel began by telling the inspector about her discovery of the destroyed library the previous night. She told how she had been unable to sleep and had sat up reading. When she spoke about the sounds, she began to shiver, and the inspector put his arm around her shoulders, saying nothing, waiting until the shivers passed. His own daughter was a little older than this girl, but he wasn't sure if she would be so calm if she was in a similar situation.

Rachel finished in a rush, telling him about the noise outside her door, the scratching, the handle turning, then the pounding.

She didn't tell him about the figure she'd seen running from the house. The figure with red hair. She didn't want to make any wild accusations. And, besides, how could it have got from the second floor to the ground so quickly?

The police didn't leave until the early afternoon. When they left, they posted one of the local constables in a car parked in the driveway.

"The car will drive off around eight or so – just when the shift changes," Michael Feeney explained to Robert Stone. "Under cover of darkness, I'll return to the house, while my men will stake out the grounds. When they come, we'll have them."

"Are you sure they'll come?"

The police officer shrugged. "They're getting braver – they'll be back. And when they do, we'll be waiting for them. Don't worry, Mr Stone, if everything goes according to plan, your troubles will be over tonight."

16

RACHEL HAD SPENT MOST OF THE MORNING watching the red-haired girl and her brother from her bedroom window. She couldn't shake off the feeling that they were somehow involved in the mysterious and terrifying events of the past few days. And last night, when she had looked from her window, the figure she had glimpsed – the red-haired figure – could easily have been Maeve or her brother, Madoc.

As they worked in the stables, the two brushed past one another without speaking, or even looking at one another, and Rachel got the impression that they had been arguing. She also noticed that the boy was walking with a slight limp.

Rachel was just about to leave her post by the window to get something to drink, when she saw the girl come up behind the boy and grab his arm. He struggled to free himself, but Maeve held on tightly, then dragged him into the nearest stable. Without thinking, Rachel leapt to her feet and dashed down the stairs. She ran out through the French doors in the dining room, cutting around to the right so that she could come at the stables from the rear. She was desperately trying to work out which stable they'd gone into, when the sound of raised voices stopped her. She was still too far away to make out what they were saying, but the tone was angry and aggressive.

They were in the last stable on the right.

Rachel went around behind the stables, picking her way through the long grass and stepping around the rusting hulk of a piece of farm machinery that had corroded into an unrecognisable mass. The voices were clearer now. She stopped, smiling slightly. Maeve had said that her brother didn't speak

– why had she lied? What was she trying to hide?

She stepped forward – and barked her shin on a piece of metal hidden in the grass. Biting her lip to keep from crying out, she hobbled over to the stable wall and, leaning back against it, examined her leg. It was scraped raw and badly bruised. But she suddenly forgot the pain when she realised that now that she was up against the wall, the voices were clearer. They were speaking some foreign language.

The girl edged forwards, until she was directly beneath the small square window set high in the barn. Maeve's voice was hard and angry, words spitting out in a musical, almost sing-song language. The second voice was male, softer, quieter, almost a whisper, and his replies were usually nothing more than single words. Were they speaking Irish? Rachel knew there was an Irish language, she occasionally heard it on the radio, but she thought it was mainly confined to the west, north and south of Ireland, in Irish speaking districts called Gaeltachts. She didn't think there were any Gaeltachts in Kildare, on the borders of Dublin.

There was a sudden sharp sound, like a slap, and then the boy's voice, speaking English now in a thick accent, each word distinct and precise. "Leave them be."

Instinct made Rachel duck – just as Madoc walked past the end of the stables heading out towards the fields. She could clearly see the imprint of a hand, red against his pale skin. Moments later Maeve appeared, running after the boy, calling his name, "Madoc ... Madoc!" He ignored her and strode on. Maeve stopped, her hands on her hips, glaring after her brother, then turned and strode away, her complexion almost as red as her hair.

Without a second thought, Rachel Stone set off after the boy, hoping he wouldn't turn around.

The boy slipped through a gap in the hedge – and

disappeared. Rachel raced across the field, pushed through the hedge and discovered that a low ditch ran alongside it. She was just in time to see Madoc's red hair disappear off to the right. Holding tightly onto the hedge, she carefully lowered herself into the ditch. It was deeper than she expected and smelt of sweet decay, rotting vegetation, wild onions and cow dung. She guessed that during the winter, the bottom of the ditch would fill with water.

Twigs snapped and crackled underfoot as she continued after Madoc, branches and brambles tugging at her clothing, snagging in her hair. She wished she'd worn her riding boots.

The ditch followed the line of bushes which wound their way across the field behind the house. She caught occasional glimpses of Madoc, but he didn't seem to notice her as he pushed on with his head bent and shoulders hunched; and although she couldn't see them, she guessed that his hands were dug deep into his pockets.

What had he and Maeve been fighting about? And why had she struck him?

A small wood loomed up. Rachel stopped and looked back. She was surprised to discover how far she'd come from the house. She could just about make out the tops of the chimneys, but they were very distant. She wavered between pressing on or going back. When she looked back over her shoulder, Madoc had disappeared, but she knew he was heading towards the trees.

With a deep sigh, Rachel continued on after the boy: she hadn't come this far just to give up.

The ditch stopped abruptly in a ragged bundle of leaves and rotten vegetation. The girl hauled herself out, wincing as her sore leg protested, and looked around. Where had Madoc gone? She was standing at the edge of the wood, the trees rising dark and gloomy directly in front of her. It was cool and damp beneath the trees and she shivered, folding her arms across her chest as she looked around. The girl tilted her head to one side, listening intently, but it was deathly silent in the wood. Crouching, she examined the hard earth around the ditch, but when she'd clambered out, she'd obviously destroyed all traces that Madoc might have left behind.

She straightened, and dusted off her hands. All right then, so she'd lost him. She really should return to the house and maybe try to follow him again tomorrow. But there was no guarantee that she'd be able to do this tomorrow. The way her father was talking, she mightn't even be in the country tomorrow. And she'd certainly be sent home if the police failed to find the people who were terrorising them.

This was the only chance she was going to get.

A twig snapped in the heart of the wood, the noise like a gunshot in the heavy silence. Rachel's head turned towards the sound, and she immediately set off in that direction.

She soon realised that she was following a barely visible path through the trees, a twisting trail that could only be an animal track. In places the undergrowth almost covered the track, but if she looked at it closely, she found bent and twisted branches, leaves knocked off branches – evidence that someone had passed this way. She stopped once, looking out through the trees to where she could just about make out the shape of a building in the middle of a field. With a start, she realised it was the burnt-out barn ... and then she put two and two together and realised that this was the same clump of trees the red-haired boy had run into that morning when he'd frightened her horse. Because she had come at the wood from another angle she hadn't immediately recognised it. She moved on more confidently now, convinced that things were beginning to fall into place.

The sudden sound of a voice stopped her. It was coming

from directly in front of her and then, sharp and clear on the cool, damp air, she smelt the odour of cigarettes.

She moved ahead more cautiously now, testing each footstep before she put her weight on it, not wanting to give away her presence in the wood.

The voices were louder now, the tang of smoke heavier. She breathed it in. It was more like cigar or pipe smoke, rather than cigarette, a heavy, sweet, woody odour. She caught a flash of red and realised that she'd found Madoc. Dropping down to the ground, she crept forward.

The ground dipped away before her into a deep natural hollow. In the centre of the hollow a small pool of water lay like a metal coin, flat and unmoving. Beyond it, the tumble-down remains of an old cottage were almost concealed by the vegetation. Part of the roof was missing and the gable wall had collapsed into a pile of stones. A twisted sycamore grew in the centre of the doorway.

Rachel realised then that the smoke she was smelling was neither cigar nor pipe smoke. Short, furry brown logs had been piled up over a low fire. It was what the Irish called turf.

Madoc was seated on a stump of wood behind the fire, mumbling quietly to himself in sing-song Irish, his head tilting from side to side, arms jerking as he spoke. Rachel watched him for a while, suddenly feeling sorry for the boy. He was big and strong, a mop of curly red hair framing a handsome face. Even from a distance she could see that his eyes were a bright vivid green. And he was obviously a little retarded. She looked at him, wondering if this was the solution to the mystery; was it nothing more than a simple boy clumsily attempting to drive away the newcomers? Maybe that's why Maeve had struck him; maybe she'd discovered the truth and had been angry because of what he'd done. After all, if the Stones left, people like Maeve and Summers would lose their jobs.

Rachel was edging away from the lip of the hollow when the boy looked up, his eyes, green and flashing, staring directly at her. In a soft voice, barely above a whisper, he spoke with a gentle Irish accent. "Why don't you come down here? We need to talk, you and I, Miss Rachel Stone."

17

"I KNOW YOU'RE THERE." The boy raised his hand and pointed directly at her. He threw back his head, nostrils flaring as he breathed in. "I can smell your perfume."

Rachel Stone came slowly to her feet. She stood on the edge of the hollow and looked down at the boy. Her every instinct was telling her to run, but instead, she said, "I was told you didn't speak."

The boy thought about it for a moment, then he smiled, showing strong yellow teeth. "There are not many people I choose to talk to."

Rachel's thoughts were racing. She felt that she was very close to something here, that the boy would be able to answer a lot of her questions. She also realised how dangerous her own situation was. She was alone in the midst of a wood, miles from the house, with a boy whose nickname was Mad Dog, whom she suspected of being involved with vandalising the house. She knew if she'd any sense, she'd turn and run, tell the police what she suspected, what she'd seen. "What do you want to talk to me about?" she asked.

The boy sat down again. "Come down," he called, "I prefer not to shout what I have to say."

Rachel remained standing on the edge of the hollow.

The boy looked up, thick bushy eyebrows raised in surprise. "Do you fear me?" He seemed to find the idea almost amusing. "I won't harm you. If I wanted to do you harm, I could have done so from the moment you crept up outside the stables."

"You knew I was there?" Rachel asked in astonishment. Then she gasped in surprise as the ground crumbled away beneath her feet and she slid down into the hollow in a cascade of stone and dirt.

Madoc remained seated.

She came to her feet and dusted herself off. "How did you know I was hiding behind the stables?" she demanded.

Madoc shrugged. "I smelt you," he said simply, nostrils flaring as he spoke. "I allowed you to follow me across the fields into the ditch. When I thought you were about to return to the house –" he lifted a stick and snapped it in two – "I called you." He stood up and stretched his hand out over the flames. "I am Madoc."

Rachel was so surprised that she reached forward and grasped his hand, feeling the strength in his grip, blinking in surprise when she felt the soft hair on the calloused palm. She had never heard of anyone having hair on the palm of their hands before. "I'm Rachel Stone."

"I know who you are, Miss Stone," Madoc said, sitting down. "I've been watching you from the moment you arrived at Seasonstown House."

Rachel crouched down, facing Madoc. Her head was pounding and there was a fluttering in the pit of her stomach. She knew that what she was doing was not only very dangerous, but also incredibly stupid.

"You've been attacking the house," she said softly, watching Madoc intently, her eyes fixed on his face.

Madoc raised his head, his bright green eyes flashing, and then he simply nodded.

"Why?" Rachel asked, "for God's sake, why?"

"I was trying to drive you away."

"Why? What have we ever done to you?" she demanded angrily.

Madoc laughed quietly, a soft sighing sound. "Nothing. I have nothing against you or your family."

"Did you burn the barn?" she asked quickly.

She didn't expect the boy to reply, but surprisingly, he said, "Yes."

"Why?" Rachel asked again, and then immediately shook her head. Stupid question.

"To try and keep you away," Madoc said simply. "I thought if you heard about the fire you wouldn't come."

"But we came ... and so you were forced to continue," Rachel added.

Madoc smiled quickly, shyly, before nodding. "I set the fire in the barn. I slashed your water-bed while you were in the bath. I watched you sitting in the library for most of the afternoon. When you left the room for your dinner, I slipped inside and destroyed it."

"But why?" Rachel asked again, and this time it was a cry almost of pain.

"To frighten you. To scare you so much that you would run away and keep going, and never come back."

Rachel stared at the boy. He was admitting to several acts of senseless vandalism, to having caused tens of thousands of dollars worth of damage, and yet he spoke so calmly, without a trace of remorse. "Why are you telling me this?" she whispered. Was he telling her because he had no intention of allowing her to leave? What was he going to do with her?

Madoc didn't move. "I'm telling you because my methods have failed. Now I need to try something different."

"You know I can go to the police with what you've told me," Rachel said very softly, wondering if he was going to attack her. She closed her hands into fists with the second knuckle slightly extended. She had attended twelve weeks of self-defence lessons because her mother had insisted. Now, she wished she'd paid more attention of the tiny Korean instructor.

"You can go to the police if you wish. But let me talk to you for a few minutes. Let me explain something ... and if you wish to go to the police then, well, I'll even come with you."

The girl thought about it for a moment, then nodded quickly. She sat down on a moss-covered tree stump across from the boy, watching him closely. He was unlike any other boy she knew. There was an incredible stillness about him, and he stared at her with a strange unblinking intensity. Leaning forward, he rested his elbows on his knees and clasped his big hands before him.

"You and your family are in great danger here," he said quietly.

Rachel nodded, unsure what to say.

"You must leave Seasonstown House and never come back."

"Why?" the girl demanded, anger creeping into her voice.

Madoc smiled, showing his teeth. "I am not your enemy, Miss Stone."

"What are you then?" she snapped. "You come into my house, you terrify me and my parents, you destroy our property ... and now you tell me that you're not our enemy ..."

He held up his right hand, palm open, fingers splayed, and she stopped.

"It begins in the past," he said suddenly. "It begins with a curse that is nearly nine hundred years old, as you measure time."

Rachel tensed. The boy was mad. Oh, he looked sane, and he seemed rational, but he was mad, quite mad. Now he was talking about a nine-hundred-year-old curse.

"You will never have heard of Natalis," he continued.

Rachel's surprised expression betrayed her and Madoc stopped, staring intently at her.

"You *have* heard of Natalis," he said very slowly. "Where?"

101

The girl frowned. She had heard the unusual name before, and very recently, but where ...? She shook her head. "I don't know," she began, "but I heard it mentioned or read about it ..." She stopped.

This day, the Thirty-First of October, All-Hallows Eve, the clan of Natalis came.

Madoc had been reading the expressions that flitted across her face. "You remember. Where did you hear the name?"

"I read about it," Rachel said slowly, "in one of the books in the library you destroyed."

The boy nodded, encouraging her to go on.

"It was the diary of someone called Piers de Courtney." Madoc lowered his head, so she wouldn't see the strange expression that flashed into his eyes. "The last entry in the diary," she continued, "said that on All-Hallows Eve, the clan of Natalis came." She shook her head. "I forget the year," she added.

"Seventeen hundred and eighty-nine," Madoc said very softly.

Something cold trickled down Rachel's spine. "How did you know?" she whispered.

The boy grinned and was about to speak, when his head jerked up, eyes wide, nostrils flaring. She started to ask a question, but he silenced her with a quick movement of his hand. He kept turning his head from side to side, listening, and she could hear him inhaling with quick, sharp sniffs. When he looked back at her, his face was pale, his red hair and green eyes now startling and vivid against the white flesh. "Go!" he said savagely, "you must go. Run for the house – and don't look back."

Rachel stood. "What is it?" she asked, her voice trembling.

"Go!" Madoc snarled. "I'll meet you back at the house, if I can." He suddenly reached forward, caught her arm and pushed her away from him. "Now go, go quickly."

His obvious fear was infectious, and Rachel found herself running through the darkening wood, concentrating hard on the track before her, knowing that she could easily slip and fall, or twist an ankle on an exposed root, or run headlong into a branch.

And while she ran she was trying to listen to the sounds around her. But the only noises she could hear were the pounding of her feet on the hard earth, the snap of branches, the swish of grass, and the thumping of her own heart.

When she reached the edge of the wood, she slowed and finally stopped, her breathing coming in great heaving gasps, searing her throat. Her lungs felt as if they were on fire, and her legs were rubbery. Doubling over, she put her hands on her knees and breathed deeply, wincing as pain stitched into her side.

It was a trick. Nothing more than a trick. Madoc had been so convincing. For a moment there she'd really believed that there was something in the wood. She shook her head, strands of blond hair curling over her eyes. She shoved them back with an angry gesture. The poor boy obviously lived in some sort of dream world, hearing voices and sounds that were all too real to him.

With a sigh, Rachel straightened, and looked out over the fields towards the house. Lights were already beginning to burn in some of the lower windows. She'd better be getting back. If her mother or father even knew she'd strayed so far from the house, there would be war.

Wood snapped behind her.

Rachel turned and looked back through the trees. But the twilight had plunged the centre of the woods into deep shadow and she could only see a few feet ahead of her.

"Madoc?" she called abruptly, annoyed at the quaver in her voice. "Madoc, is that you?"

A flash of red off to her right.

"Madoc!" she shouted, angry now. This was obviously part of his game. She saw the flicker of red again, close to the ground, still off to the right.

"Run, Rachel, run!" Madoc's voice, high and terrified ... and coming from the left.

She spun around to the right. The red shape was still in the trees, twisting, turning, darting from shadow to shadow ... always edging closer.

Rachel Stone turned and ran.

Twilight had turned the fields gloomy and indistinct and she could just about make out the opening in the hedge where the ditch ran on the far side of the field. Her feet pounded across the ground, long grass hissing and whispering against her legs. She thought she heard Madoc's voice again, shouting, but she couldn't be sure.

Wood snapped again, louder, closer.

And then an animal howled.

The sound was terrifying, the savage snarl of a large dog. And it was close, so close. She heard it then, panting, padding behind her, the rhythm of its paws beating off the ground as it bounded after her.

They had set a dog on her! Rachel ran even harder. Her every breath was agony; there was fire in her lungs, acid in her belly, a dagger-like stitch in her right side that caused her to stagger.

The snuffling, panting was right behind her.

Through tear-filled eyes she could see the lights of the house. It was much nearer. If she could just reach the gap in the hedge, someone was sure to see her from the house, and if she could scream, even once, then they'd come and everything would be all right, and ...

The ground vanished beneath her and she fell headlong into the ditch. Ignoring the pain of bruised flesh and scraped skin, she staggered to her feet, and looked up.

The beast's head appeared over the edge of the ditch. She had a fleeting impression of coarse red hair, hard green eyes and ragged teeth, before the animal leapt into the ditch on top of her.

18

SEAN SUMMERS'S FACE WAS PALE and sweat glistened on his bald skull. "I've searched every room in the house from top to bottom. There's no sign of her."

Elizabeth Stone looked at Robert, her eyes wide and terrified. Her husband put his arm around his wife's shoulders and squeezed comfortingly. But he had no words for her.

Detective Inspector Michael Feeney came through the French windows, dusting off his hands. Inspector Lanigan followed more slowly. "Nothing," Feeney said quietly. "We've searched the grounds, the outhouses, barns and stables. We've shouted ourselves hoarse. Your daughter's not here."

"Where is she?" Elizabeth asked quietly. "She's been kidnapped, hasn't she?"

Feeney didn't answer the question directly. "We've set up road-blocks. Police headquarters in Dublin have been informed."

"What do we do now?" Robert Stone asked the police inspector.

"Now we wait, Sir. The next move is all theirs."

THE SMELL BROUGHT RACHEL STONE AWAKE, a foul, bitter odour, a mixture of rot and urine, a sickly sweet smell that she instantly associated with disease and the musty odour of animal sweat.

Before she opened her eyes, she attempted to work out where she was. She was lying on a cold wooden floor, the wood rough against her cheek, with her hands and legs securely tied. Her fingers were tingling with pins and needles. Water dripped monotonously close by, the sound hollow and plinking, and there was a rattling, hissing sound in the distance, but there were no other noises in the room.

Panic bubbled up inside her, shuddering up from deep within her stomach, flooding her mouth with a sour liquid. She swallowed hard. Panicking wasn't going to help. She had to stay very calm now. She didn't know how long she'd been unconscious – her last memories were of the terrifying dog looming up over the edge of the ditch and then leaping forward. She must have fainted. It was twilight then, and she'd been away from the house for a long time. So, at the very least, she would have been missed by now, and the police would be looking for her. Maybe Madoc had gone to the house and told her parents what had happened.

The girl opened her eyes.

There was a single moment of panic when she thought she couldn't see, but then her eyes adjusted and she could just about make out a thin grey line beneath a distant door. The thick blackness overhead shifted into a couple of lighter patches with tiny white spots in them. It took her a few moments to make sense of what she was seeing, but then she suddenly realised that she was lying on her back, looking up through a roof that had holes in it. She was looking at the night sky, speckled with stars. She realised then that the rattling and hissing she was hearing was the wind blowing through trees, disturbing leaves, rubbing branches together. Did that mean she was still in the wood?

Taking a deep breath, Rachel Stone opened her mouth and screamed.

Footsteps clattered on bare floorboards, and then the door crashed open. Monstrous shadows moved in dancing candle-light. She caught a glimpse of red hair before she was roughly hauled to her feet and slammed up against a wall with enough force to knock the wind from her. When she opened her eyes, she found herself staring into Maeve Alton's grass-green eyes. There were three other people in the room, all holding candles. In the flickering light, Maeve's face was a twisted ugly mask.

"I told them to gag you, but they were afraid you'd choke and die. And we don't want you to die – not just yet, anyway," she added with a smirk.

Rachel's lips worked, but no sound came out.

"Save your questions. You'll get all the answers you want in a little while." She stroked Rachel's face with her long-fingered hands. "Now, be patient. Everything comes to him who waits ..." She began to laugh then, a high-pitched wild sound, and the others in the room joined in. Rachel squeezed her eyes shut, twisting her head from side to side, trying to cut out the terrifying sound, but it just went on and on, gradually melting into a long continuous howl.

When she awoke again, the moon was high in the sky, shining through the broken ceiling, bathing portions of the room in a cold white light. Rolling over, Rachel dug her heels in and levered herself into a sitting position and looked around the room.

There was a shape in the corner.

Rachel squinted into the shadows. She was too tired to be frightened anymore. "Who are you?"

Claws clicked on the bare floorboards as a huge hound padded out of the shadows.

The girl felt her breath catch in her throat. It was the dog that had chased her. The animal was enormous. She didn't recognise the breed. It looked like a cross between an Alsatian and a wolf. Its head was broad and long-snouted, its cold green eyes regarded her unblinkingly, and its long-haired coat was a deep rich red. Long strands of white saliva drooled from its open teeth-filled jaws.

Rachel swallowed hard. "Good boy," she whispered hoarsely.

The dog turned and padded to the door. With a long-nailed claw, it batted at the door, opening it, and slipped out. She heard its claws clicking on floorboards and then the sound of the animal descending down bare stairs. There were sounds of distant snarls, and an answering bark, and Rachel realised that there was more than one dog in the house.

Where was Madoc?

She drew her legs in under her and rose slowly to her feet. Although her feet were tied at the ankle, she could take tiny mincing steps. Now that her eyes had adjusted to the gloom, she could just about make out the rectangular shape of a boarded-up window directly ahead of her. Even as she squinted at it, moonlight, white and silver, washed over the wood, painting the cracks in light. If she could peer through those cracks, she might be able to see where she was.

She fell once as she crossed the room, crashing to the floor, numbing the entire left side of her body. Coloured lights danced before her eyes, and there was a deep, bell-like ringing in her ears. She lay on the floor, expecting that the door would burst open and that the huge dogs or their owners would come running in. But there was no movement on the stairs, and she heard nothing from the rooms below.

Had they left?

Maybe they had gone to Seasonstown House. But, since she hadn't heard the sound of a car starting up, that meant that the house must be reasonably close by. The thought spurred her on. Rolling over onto her stomach, she drew her knees in beneath her and rose, first into a squatting position, then upright. She didn't know how long she had before they returned, but she didn't want to be here when they got back. Whoever they were.

With a mixture of tiny steps and little jumps, Rachel approached the window. The moon had gone behind a cloud, shifting the room back into darkness. But her eyes had adjusted to the dark, and she could make out vague shapes: a table, two broken-backed chairs, a bed beneath the window.

The sickly sweet smell was stronger here. The odour reminded her of rotten fruit and stagnant ponds.

Her knees bumped against the bed. Reluctant to climb up onto the mattress – God alone knows what might be living in it – she leaned forward, squinting to peer through the boards across the window.

There were lights in the distance. Rachel moved her head, trying to make sense of what she was seeing. More lights appeared, and with a start she realised she was looking at Seasonstown House in the distance. Two bright lights shone across the front of the house as a car drove up.

If she could just get free, she could make a run for it. And if she screamed, her cries would carry on the night air.

Moonlight suddenly washed over the distant house, turning it silver and black. The brilliant light slatted through the boarded-up window, throwing a zebra pattern across the bed and floor.

Something moved in the bed, making the pattern ripple. The odour of decay intensified, catching at the girl's throat, making her eyes water.

She was backing away from the bed, when the shape sat up and grabbed her arm. Before she could scream, a voice spoke, wheezing out from the darkness.

"Don't think you can leave us, little one. There is nowhere for you to run. You must stay with us a little longer." There was a rasping breath. "It will end soon enough and you will be free then."

THE CRASH BROUGHT THEM ALL TO THEIR FEET. Robert Stone took a step closer to the door, but Elizabeth caught his arm, pulling him back. The door immediately swung open and Detective Inspector Feeney stepped into the room. There was a big dark pistol in his hand. "Stay here. Whatever happens; whatever you hear – stay here!"

They both nodded.

The inspector stepped back out into the hall, pulling the door closed behind him. They could hear running feet, and quickly whispered orders.

Then silence.

"It came from upstairs," Elizabeth said, her voice barely above a whisper.

Robert Stone nodded. Unconsciously he raised his eyes and looked at the ceiling. The noise had come from Rachel's room.

There was a sudden shout from outside, followed by the flat bang of a shot-gun. Three sharper cracks followed, but these came from upstairs. Footsteps thundered down the stairs and along the hall, heels clicking on the marble. There were shouts, and then a searchlight flashed across the window.

"What's happening?" Elizabeth asked.

"Maybe they've got someone," Robert said. He was turning towards the door as it opened and the tall police inspector returned. He was pushing fat copper-coloured bullets into his revolver.

"What happened?" Robert Stone demanded.

The inspector sat down with a sigh. "There was someone upstairs ... in your daughter's room. One of my men heard a noise and went to investigate. But when he stepped into Rachel's room he was hit hard on the back of the head by a blunt instrument. The noise we heard was him hitting the floor. When I got up there the room was a mess, clothes shredded, the mattress torn apart, feathers from the pillow everywhere."

"How did they get into the house?" Robert asked. "The servants have all been sent home. There's only your people and us here."

"The window was open," the inspector said quietly.

"But it's three floors up," Robert protested.

The inspector nodded. "I know. When I leaned out the window, someone was climbing down the wall." Before he could be asked any more questions, he hurried on. "I shouted for them to stop. They ignored me and then either jumped or fell about ten feet to the ground. One of my men let off a shot-gun, and then I fired three times. I saw two of the bullets strike sparks off the ground, but I think I may have hit them with the third shot. I could swear they were running bent over when I saw them."

"But why?" Elizabeth demanded. "What where they doing in Rachel's room?"

The inspector ran a hand through his dark hair. "I don't know, Mrs Stone," he said truthfully. He reached into his pocket and lifted out a broken brown board. "Does either of you recognise this?" Robert took the board from the inspector's hands and looked at it, turning it over before handing it across to his wife. "It's a book binding," she said, "like the ones that were destroyed in the library yesterday." She handed it back to the inspector. "Where did you get it?"

"On the ground outside your daughter's window," Inspector Feeney said softly, looking at the broken binding again. "It was dropped by whoever broke into your daughter's room."

"Why?" Robert and Elizabeth Stone asked together.

The police officer shook his head. "I don't know, but it must have been very precious for someone to take the risk and return here for it."

"But it doesn't bring us any closer to finding Rachel," Elizabeth said bitterly.

"But it does, Ma'am. It tells us that your daughter must be close ... very close indeed."

Saturday, 31st October

21

THE SHOTS ECHOED ACROSS THE STILL NIGHT AIR. The figure on the bed shuddered, flinching with each brittle sound, and sank back into the shadows, releasing Rachel's hand.

The girl stumbled away from the bed, heart hammering in her chest, a roaring in her ears.

The hand that had wrapped itself around her arm had been twisted into an ugly claw, the hairy flesh pale, blotched and diseased-looking in the moonlight. The nails had been long and black.

Rachel backed up against the wall, still staring at the dark shape on the bed. She was thankful that she couldn't make out any details, but in the silence following the shots she could hear the wheezing gasps for breath.

Claws clicked on the stairs and the door creaked open. An enormous evil-eyed hound padded into the room, crossed the floor and sat beside the bed. The moonlight lent its fur a dull sheen, giving it an almost ghostly appearance. Against the shadows, its teeth were very white.

Another dog entered the room, immediately followed by two more. They were all the same breed. The three dogs joined the first at the bed. Their heads turned to look at her, their eyes flat and silver, but what she found even more terrifying was that they made no sound.

There were muffled shouts from below and a dog barked twice. Footsteps – many footsteps – pounded on the stairs and across the landing, and suddenly it seemed as if the room was filling with people and dogs. Three more dogs padded into the room and took up position beside the bed, and then four people entered, two of them supporting a fifth who was limping badly.

A match flared with the quick sharp smell of sulphur, and a candle was lit. Milky light danced around the crowded room, across pale human flesh and red animal fur. Two more candles were lit, creating pools of warm light in the centre of the room, but leaving the corners in shadow.

The candle-light ran on red hair, and Rachel discovered that the four people – two men, two women – who had entered the room all had red hair, and were obviously related. Stepping back, they allowed the injured person they had been helping to come closer to her. It was Maeve Alton, her face twisted in pain, sweat shining wetly on her forehead. She was clutching a sheaf of yellow pages which she shook at Rachel. "You'll never know how close you came ..." she whispered.

The girl shook her head. "I don't know what you're talking about."

"Oh, I think you do," Maeve said coldly. "I heard you talking to Madoc. I heard him tell you about the clan of Natalis; I heard you say you had read about it in a book." She lifted the pages again, and Rachel caught a glimpse of the old faded writing. It was the book she'd taken from the library; the cover was missing. Maeve carried it across to the bed, passing it into the shadows.

"She knows about us. I was afraid if the book remained in the house one of the others might read it too ..."

"I don't know who these Natalis people are," Rachel said loudly. She looked at the other people in the room, but their eyes were in shadow, their faces expressionless. "You've got to believe me!"

"I believe you."

The voice was the same hoarse whisper she had heard earlier. Everyone immediately turned to look over towards the

117

deeply shadowed bed.

Rachel looked into the dark corner, straining to make out the shape of the person lying in the bed. "I read the name for the first time yesterday. I came across it in the diary of someone called Piers de Courtney. He said that the clan of Natalis was coming."

"They came," the voice rasped.

Rachel frowned. "He was writing ... "

"... on All-Hallows Eve, in the year of Our Lord, Seventeen Hundred and Eighty-Nine," the voice finished.

"Was he a relation?" Rachel asked quietly.

There was a wheezing laugh. "Oh yes, you could say that."

"Who are you?" the girl asked. "What do you want with me? Why were you trying to frighten my family away?"

A quick murmur ran around the room. "We were not trying to frighten you away." There was a deep rasping breath that ended in a liquid gurgling sound. "Oh no, on the contrary. We wanted you to stay. In fact, that's why we've taken you: to make sure that your family remains in the house for another few hours. That's all we need ... just another few hours."

"Who are you ...?"

There was no answer, but Rachel got the impression that some unseen signal had been given by the person in the shadows. Without a word, two of the men left the room, their footsteps echoing and re-echoing along the landing and down the stairs. A door slammed, and there was a muffled shout, and then Rachel heard the footsteps returning, and the sound of something heavy being dragged along the floor, accompanied by the tiniest of metallic jingles.

"We wanted you to stay," the wheezing voice said suddenly, startling her. The door opened and the two red-haired men returned. They were half-carrying, half-dragging the still body of a red-haired boy between them. Heavy padlocked chains had been wrapped around his chest and legs. Even before they raised his head, Rachel knew it was Madoc.

"We wanted you to stay," the voice repeated, "but Madoc was trying to drive you away."

"Madoc?" Rachel whispered, completely confused now.

"Madoc thought he was trying to protect you. But Madoc forgot that his first loyalty is to his family, to his clan."

"Why was he trying to drive us away from the house?" Rachel asked.

Madoc raised his head and looked at the girl. There was a bruise on the side of his jaw and his right eye was half closed. "Why don't you ask them why they wanted you to stay?" he whispered. Maeve snarled something in Irish, and although Rachel didn't understand the words, she could guess what they meant. Shut up!

"Tell me why you wanted my family to remain in the house," Rachel said quietly.

A long-fingered, black-nailed hand appeared out of the shadows. It was clutching the ragged remains of the old diary. "Do you know what day today is?" the rasping voice whispered.

She thought about it. It was Friday ... no, surely it was after midnight? It was now Saturday, the thirty-first of ... "Hallowe'en," she murmured.

"The night of the October Moon. The night when the veil between this and the Otherworld is stretched to its limit. The dead walk tonight, the banshee howls, and the *sidhe*, the Shining Folk who once ruled this land, ride out on their steeds, taking all they meet. Tonight is a time of great power, of great magic. On the night of the October Moon a spell may be cast ... or an ancient curse lifted."

Rachel glanced sidelong at Madoc. He too had spoken of an ancient curse.

119

"You've gone quiet, girl. Don't you believe me?" the rasping voice sounded surprised.

"I think you're trying to scare me," Rachel said loudly. "And you still haven't answered Madoc's question. Why are you trying to keep my family in the house?"

The black-nailed hands slowly turned the pages of the book. When the voice spoke again, it was soft, barely above a whisper. "This day, the Thirty-First of October, All-Hallows Eve, the clan of Natalis came." The book was closed, the diseased and twisted claw-like hands folded over it. "Do you keep a diary, Rachel Stone?" the voice asked, surprising her.

"No, not any more," she answered.

"A pity. But perhaps after tonight you will start one. And you too can begin with the entry, 'This day, the Thirty-First of October, All-Hallows Eve, the clan of Natalis came.'"

Rachel shook her head in frustration. "You're not making any sense. You're not answering any of my questions. Who are you, and what has this Natalis family to do with anything?"

The figure in the bed sat forward, the candlelight flowing across its face. It was an old man, his features incredibly wrinkled, milky green eyes sunk deep into skin the colour of old leather. Strands of pale red hair clung to his flaking scalp. But it was his teeth that caught Rachel's terrified gaze. They were the ragged fangs of a dog. His hand moved, gesturing to the people in the room. "We are the clan of Natalis." The old man bared the fangs in a terrifying smile. "I am Piers de Courtney." He lifted the torn yellowed pages. "This is my diary."

Rachel felt as if the breath had been knocked from her body. "But that's impossible," she breathed. "That would make you ..."

"I was born in the year of Our Lord seventeen hundred and seventy-two. I was ten and seven years when the clan of Natalis came. That was two hundred and three years ago!"

Rachel was shaking her head from side to side. They were trying to frighten her. "Impossible," she snapped. "Humans don't live that long."

The old man began to laugh, and then slowly, one by one the rest of the people in the room joined in. Even the dogs began to howl. "Don't you realise the truth, girl? We are the clan of Natalis. And the clan of Natalis are no longer human: that is our curse." The old man's voice had risen to a ragged screech. "But tonight the curse ends. Tonight, the night of the October Moon, we will pass this curse on to your family!"

22

•

"IT BEGINS," PIERS DE COURTNEY SAID, "not two hundred years ago, but long before that. A holy man, Giraldus Cambrensis, recorded the legend of this clan in the year of Our Lord eleven hundred and eighty-five ... but the tale was ancient even then.

"It begins with the Abbot Natalis, a holy man, a follower of the bishop men know today as Patrick." De Courtney held up a strip of thick curling manuscript. "Natalis too kept a diary of sorts. Listen, then, to the legend of the clan of Natalis ..."

This is truly a land of terrors.

There are times when I am convinced that God does not show his face in this place. Even on the warmest summer's day it is cold; it rains every day, and the wind that blows from the Northlands is icy. Many of my brothers have died of the sickness brought on by the weather, and although I am still considered a young man, I can feel the stiffness in my bones, the aching in my joints.

But Patrick, who was amongst the first to bring the Word of God to this terrible place, had survived this and worse, and it is his example that keeps me going.

One hundred and twenty days have passed since I set foot on Hibernia. The natives – a crude and savage race – call it Ierne and Erin and Eriu, and a dozen other barbarous names, but I think I prefer a name I learnt in my studies in Rome: on the charts there it was referred to as the Island at the Edge of the World. I thought then that it was just a fanciful name, such as mariners give to uncharted islands, but now that I have lived in this place, I realise that there is much truth in it. The world ends beyond this island's western coast. The sea foams down into limitless space ... and who knows what creatures may crawl up from that place?

That would certainly account for the wonders and terrors I have seen on this isle.

This land is haunted. The dead walk and talk and are accepted by the people as a normal part of their everyday life. At night, the silence is rent by the wailing of the fairy woman who calls for death. The pooka gallops across the thickly forested countryside. Although it is usually in the shape of a horse, it must be the devil's steed. I have seen with my own eyes the ghost-white balls of fire that hover over the marshlands; many a man has followed those ... and never been seen again. The pagan peoples here speak of the Little People and the Shining Folk, they talk of magical islands, of villages hidden deep beneath the ground or at the bottom of lakes. And some of these lakes are infested with the terrifying *peist*, which is sometimes described as a dragon, or as a serpent – though there are no serpents here in Hibernia, for Bishop Patrick had banished them in the first days of his ministry here.

The people here follow a primitive pagan faith and though some have converted to the One True Religion, many have not, preferring to keep to the religion their forefathers worshipped. Those who leave their pagan religion to be converted risk the hatred of their own clan, and the curses of their priests, who are themselves powerful magicians. I have seen strong and healthy men sicken and die because they believed themselves cursed by these priests.

Only a fool would challenge these priests.

I was that fool.

This is the land they call Ossory. It is a dark place, deeply wooded, the sun rarely penetrating to the forest floor. The clans live deep in the heart of the forest, coming out at night to raid neighbouring clans, stealing slaves and cattle and then retreating into the wooded fortresses.

I was warned not to come to this place. The old religion is very strong here, and so far none of the clansmen has converted to the Word of God. Many of the brothers who had gone before me had been martyred because of their faith. But I felt it was my duty ... and perhaps I thought that I would succeed where so many others had failed. Does that make me guilty of the sin of pride? I suppose it does.

Colum, one of the Northern tribesmen who converted to the One True Religion and who now follows me, translating and attempting to teach me the barbarous language, accompanied me into this land of Ossory. Though he was plainly fearful, he put his trust in God, and led me through the winding forest tracks. The most powerful clan in this province lives deep in the heart of the forest. Colum said if I could convert their chieftain, the clan would follow, and then all the other clans would follow their example.

I kept my head down as we moved deeper and deeper into the forest. We were following a trail that was little more than an animal track. It was riddled with holes and overgrown with roots and twisting vines upon which a man might easily twist or break an ankle, and such a minor injury could often prove fatal.

Close to noon, I stopped to cut an entangling briar off my cloak. I had been talking to Colum, practising the barbaric Irish language, when I suddenly realised that he hadn't replied to a question. When I looked up, he had vanished.

I stopped, feeling my heart begin to hammer in my chest. I was about to call out when I saw movement in the bushes off to my right. I took a deep breath, smiling with relief – when the bushes parted with a whispering rustle and a great flame-haired warrior stepped out onto the path. While I was staring at him, the bushes all around me came alive with wild-haired fur-clad warriors. One pointed a metal-headed spear at me. Blood dripped from its tip.

Crossing myself, I bowed my head and prepared to die.

Their leader, a huge foul-smelling brute, came forward, moving surprisingly quietly in the thick undergrowth and stopped before me. He gestured with his spear, splashing me with hot blood. When he spoke, I could barely make out his accent.

"You are a holy man?"

"I am the Abbot Natalis ..." I began, looking the man in the eye. I remember his eyes were a vivid green.

"You follow the White Christ?" the warrior demanded.

I bowed.

The man showed his teeth in a savage smile. He gestured with his head and two warriors came up behind me and caught my arms, actually lifting me off the ground.

"How strong is your god?" he demanded.

"Strong," I said quickly.

"Stronger than the ancient gods of Erin? Stronger than the Dadga and Danu?"

"Yes," I said proudly.

"We shall see," he said. "Bring him." He took three steps away from me and vanished into the forest.

The remainder of my journey was a confusion of being hauled through dense forest, of snapping branches, clinging vines and stinging briars. I attempted to pray, but I couldn't concentrate on the words. Perhaps I lost consciousness.

I remember however, when the forest ended abruptly and a sizeable village appeared. There must have been nearly twenty huts behind a high palisade of pointed stakes. As I was dragged into the village, I could see that all the villagers had come out to see me. They lined the route in silence, watching me, their faces blank and expressionless. Many of them were red-haired, and I knew that most would be blood-related.

I was thrown to the ground in front of a long wooden hut. A dozen men stood before the hut. I recognised the leader. He was still holding the blood-stained spear.

He raised his arm high. "This is a follower of the White Christ," he shouted. "He claims that his god is more powerful than ours. What say you?"

"No," they all shouted.

"What were you doing in my forest, holy man?" The chieftain made a face as he spoke the last word, almost as if it left a sour taste in his mouth.

"I was coming here. I was coming to bring you the Word of God."

The chieftain looked around at his people. "He is condemned out of his own mouth. He was coming here to bring us the word of god – but which god, not ours, no – his own weakling god. He was coming here to enchant us, to make us slaves of the White Christ."

I shook my head.

"He would have crept up to our village at dead of night and cast his spell over us. I have seen these followers of Christ. They pay homage to a chieftain who lives across the seas, but who cannot protect them. Their religion weakens them; they carry no weapons. Why, even their own prophet could not save himself!"

"But He rose again," I snapped. "He died and rose again – none of your gods can do that."

The chieftain leaned forward. "But my gods do not die!"

I took a deep breath, calming myself. Bishop Patrick had been similarly tested and questioned when he had set the

126

fire on Tara's hills. He had emerged triumphant from that encounter and had even managed to convert Angras, the Queen.

There was movement in the door of the hut behind the chieftain and a small wizened shape stepped out into the early afternoon sunlight. The man was incredibly old, his skin wrinkled and sagging, hanging about him like a badly fitting jerkin. Blue dye streaked his arms and forehead, and a dozen strings of beads and baubles hung around his neck. He was leaning on a twisted staff that was topped with a wolf's skull. When he pointed at me, I realised his fingernails were unnaturally long.

"I curse you," the old man hissed. "I curse you. I curse you," he repeated.

Thrice cursed! I knew the saying: thrice cursed is doomed.

I crossed myself and prayed, calling upon the Lord and His saints and martyrs to protect me. Finally, I remembered the special words of Patrick. He had spoken the prayer when he had been trapped, surrounded by those who would have killed him. Even during his own lifetime, the words were being called Patrick's Breastplate. I used them now.

"Let Christ walk before me ..." I looked around, "and behind me. "Let Him be beneath my feet and above me ..."

"He curses us," the old man screamed. He shook his wolf-headed staff.

"Let Him be on my right and my left sides ..."

The old man began muttering. His eyes were rolling in his head, spittle dribbling from the corner of his mouth. His left hand, twisted now into a claw was flexing over the wolf's skull.

"Let Him be with me in my waking hours, and while I sleep ..."

127

A cold blue light began playing over the wolf's skull. Tiny white sparks gathered in the hollow eye sockets, looking like winking eyes, the flames dancing along the ragged teeth.

"Let me always think of Him, and speak of Him always. And I will see and hear Him everywhere."

A glittering white fire had settled over the animal's skull. I saw the image of a snarling wolf outlined in fire and light. The fire intensified, lending it the semblance of fur. The old man had gone rigid, his left arm outstretched, fingers point- ing at me. "The wolf, our mascot, protects us," he screamed, spraying me with his spittle. "The wolf will devour your soul!"

The fiery wolf leapt off the staff, its massive body flowing out behind it.

I made the Sign of the Cross and prepared to die.

It was as if I had traced two lines of golden fire in the air. The burning cross hung quivering between me and the wolf.

The wolf struck the cross.

The explosion of fire and light threw me to the ground. The wolf dissolved into dozens of cold white sparks which spat outwards into the assembled crowd. Some buzzed into the ground around me, but the burning cross protected me.

I was looking at the chieftain as the spark struck him, resting on his cheek like a hot cinder. He slapped at it, and then stopped, looking at his hand. I saw him frown, then his eyes opened wide in horror. His hand was changing, twist- ing, altering before his gaze. The nails lengthened, curled, the fingers bent, hair sprouting visibly along the back and across the palm of his hands. He fell to the ground, shud- dering, as spasms twisted his body.

I knelt on the muddy ground, crouched in prayer, while all around me similar changes were rippling through the bodies of the villagers. Squeezing my eyes closed, I

128

attempted to shut out the terrible sounds – of snapping bones and twisting, tearing skin, of shouts that sounded like snarls, and screams that were too high-pitched to have been made by a human throat.

And then silence.

When I opened my eyes again, I was surrounded by a wolf pack. A red-haired, green-eyed wolf pack.

The old man's spell, which had been intended for me, had been turned back by the cross, cursing the entire village.

One of the huge wolves padded up to me, rubbing its great head against my leg. I knew this was the chieftain. The massive jaws worked, and although the sounds were fractured and broken, I could just about make out what the beast was saying.

"Your god is the greater, abbot. Now we are your followers, we are your children. We are the clan of Natalis ..."

"And we are the descendants of that clan," Piers de Courtney said hoarsely. "We are both men and wolves, and something in between. The humankind have a name for us – they call us werewolves."

The girl said nothing.

"Towards the end of his life, Natalis prayed to God to allow the curse to be lifted from his clan." The old man leaned forward, his long teeth flashing in the light. "But the curse could not be lifted ... except ..." he paused, "except that once in every generation, on the night of the October Moon, on the eve of Samhain, when the ancient magic of Erin regains a shadow of its former power, then the curse may be transferred, passed on to another clan who are tied to the land. Part of Seasonstown House is built upon the site of the ancient village. Whoever occupies the house can be cursed." His teeth closed with a click. "In the year seventeen hundred and eighty-nine, the werewolves came howling around Seasonstown House. We defended ourselves as best we could, but they eventually overwhelmed my family. That night my family were cursed. Those cursed with the werewolf blood bear the red hair and green eyes of the original clan of Natalis. That curse ends tonight. Tonight, we will become human again, while you and your family will become the new clan of Natalis! That is why we wanted you to stay," he finished in a ragged whisper.

23

HIGH-PITCHED, EERIE AND TERRIFYING, the howl rolled across the flat countryside. Moments later it was joined by a second and then a third.

Robert Stone stood on the lawn outside the dining room drinking a cup of strong black coffee. He tilted his head, listening. "Wolves," he said shortly.

Michael Feeney shook his head. "No, Sir, there are no wolves in Ireland. It's just some dogs from one of the local farms howling at the full moon." He jerked his chin up to where the full moon rode in the cloudy sky.

"It's wolves," Stone said decisively. "I heard them in northern Canada a couple of years ago. It's the sort of sound you never forget."

The detective didn't bother to correct the older man. There were no wolves in Ireland, hadn't been for a couple of hundred years.

The dogs howled again.

They were closer this time.

MADOC SPOKE INTO THE SILENCE. "They've gone."

Rachel turned to look at the boy. "Where have they gone?" she asked, although she already knew the answer.

"To Seasonstown House!"

When de Courtney had finished his terrifying story, Rachel and Madoc had been carried down through the dilapidated house, along stairs that creaked and cracked with every step, across a hallway which sagged beneath their weight. By the light of a single flickering candle, Rachel saw the cellar door standing open, gaping like a great mouth, but before she could even cry out, she was shoved down a short flight of stairs, and Madoc was pushed inside after her. Maeve stood in the doorway, the candle held high, casting a flickering light across the bare cellar. She smiled, her teeth yellow in the light. "We'll come back for you," she said very softly. She bent and tipped the candle, allowing a little grease to drip onto the top step, and then stuck the candle in place. "The rats come out in the dark," she whispered, "and I wouldn't want anything to eat you before I do." She turned away, slamming the door behind her. A key turned and bolts rattled into place. Then the footsteps retreated across the hall and back up the stairs.

The boy and girl sat in silence, listening to the vague noises from upstairs. A few moments later a chilling howl startled Rachel, making her jump, then it was joined by more and more howling dogs until it sounded as if a pack of wild animals was trapped in the upstairs room.

The howling stopped abruptly, then the stairs creaked as dozens of paws clicked down the bare boards, across the hall

... and then silence. The clan of Natalis had gone to Seasons-town House.

"Madoc ..." Rachel said, "what's happening?"

"Master de Courtney told you," the boy said shortly.

"But ... but what he said about ... about werewolves ... and ..."

"It was all true, Rachel," the boy said gently.

"But werewolves don't exist!"

"We do," Madoc said simply. "There is even a medical name for it: lycanthropy. There are wolf-men in the mythology of every race. It is one of the oldest legends of mankind. And in every legend there is a grain of truth. Over the years the legend has become corrupt and distorted, and your knowledge of the werewolves has been fashioned by too many bad films. We are not savage men-beasts. When we take on our wolf shape, we become true wolves ... like the beasts you saw upstairs," he added with a cold smile. "They were my cousins. Though, while we are in our beast shape, we retain our human intelligence and capacity for understanding. We don't need the light of the full moon to take our beast shape, though our power is strongest then and the transformation is easier. While we wear our human shape, we are stronger and faster than the humankind, but an ordinary bullet – not a silver one – can kill us. We are not invincible. We can be killed if our necks are broken, or our spines snapped, or a stake driven through our hearts, and fire is the great enemy of our people. But if we are only injured, we recover quickly."

His teeth flashed in a quick smile. "The night before last your father hit me in his car. A human would have died, but I survived. Tonight, Maeve was shot in the side. By dawn, there won't even be a scar. My clan don't age as quickly as your race do, though old age will claim us all eventually. Some of the original clan of Natalis survived for a thousand years and more, though most of the present clan were all living in the house in 1789 when they were bitten. Some of us – like Maeve and myself – were born into this clan. We are not so prone to disease. De Courtney was already ill when he became one of the clan of Natalis. Over the past two centuries the disease has slowly eaten through his body, but he will not die yet because the blood of the werewolf runs in his veins. He is our leader, because the leaders from ancient times died. But he is tired now, he wants to become human again. He wants to die in peace."

"How ... how old are you, Madoc?" Rachel whispered.

The candlelight crawled across the boy's face, throwing his eyes into deep shadow. He smiled, but kept his lips closed, not showing his teeth. "Don't worry, I'm only fifteen," he said. "As I said, I was born a werewolf."

Rachel jerked her head upwards. "I understand why de Courtney wants to become human again, but why do the others? I would have thought being stronger and faster, and practically immortal, would appeal to everyone."

"It is not easy to watch the world change around you. To see an entire way of life change and change and change again. It isn't easy to watch friends grown old and die, nor is it easy to be constantly moving on from place to place before people begin to wonder why you never age. And in these days of computers and birth and death records, it isn't as easy as it once was to fake a death or invent a relative." There was a long pause and then Madoc asked, "You're not sure whether to believe all this, are you? Even after all the evidence."

Rachel laughed shortly. "What evidence? Vandalism up at the house, the wild rantings of an old man, a scary ghost story."

"Rachel, listen to me," Madoc said seriously. "Tonight, the clan of Natalis will visit Seasonstown House once again. Your family – and everyone in the house – will be attacked and bitten by them. The disease is carried in our saliva; the antidote in your blood. Once bitten, your family will become werewolves on the night of the next full moon."

He smiled quickly. "They will wear the red hair and green eyes of the clan of Natalis. They will be confused, frightened and hungry ... terribly, terribly hungry. Whatever causes this change in our bodies needs fuel. The stories of werewolves killing sheep, horses – even humans – is true. Your family will wear their wolf shape that night, but with the dawn they will become human again.

"Every night for the following few weeks they will become wolves during the hours of darkness until they learn to control the were-change. They will carry this disease back to America. And it will spread like a plague that will eventually threaten the entire human race."

"That's why you tried to scare us away, isn't it?" she asked.

"I wanted it to end here. It's wrong to pass on this foul curse. If we don't spread the disease, in time the clan of Natalis will die out. The werewolves will be no more."

The girl took a deep breath. What she'd learnt tonight went contrary to everything she'd been taught. And if the werewolf legend was true, what other legends were also true ... what other beasts and creatures walked this world?

"You've got to believe me," Madoc insisted.

"I believe you," she said wearily.

The boy nodded. "The werewolves have survived for so long because no-one has believed in them."

"We've got to stop them!" Rachel said simply.

Madoc nodded. "I know that." He came to his feet and hobbled over to the girl, his chains rattling. Now that he was close, she could smell a faintly musky, though not unpleasant, odour off him. "Now, I want you to listen to me very carefully, Rachel. There is a way we can defeat the clan of Natalis, but

135

you must trust me. Whatever happens, I swear I will never harm you ..."

Crouched against the rotting wooden stairs, Rachel Stone watched Madoc in the light of the candle-stub.

Madoc sat facing her, his back to the damp cellar wall, his legs drawn up to his chest, his chained wrists draped across his knees. His head was thrown back, the candlelight turning his flesh yellow, painting the red of his hair a pale gold. Beneath his closed eyelids, she could see that his eyes were moving rapidly, darting to and fro. He shuddered, then his mouth opened wide in a huge cracking yawn, the flesh pulling back from his gums, his teeth snapping closed with an audible click.

Madoc's hands began to clench and unclench, the chains around his wrists making tiny tinkling sounds.

When Rachel looked at his face again, the transformation had begun.

The shape of his face had altered. The cheekbones were sharper, more sloping, the bones of the nose thicker, more pronounced, the lower jawbone had drawn back, leaving the upper teeth exposed. Coarse reddish bristles appeared in patches across his cheeks and forehead, growing even as she watched, pushing their way through his skin. His skin began moving, rippling ... no not the skin, but the muscles and sinews beneath the skin.

The boy began to shudder and spasm as his muscles jerked and twitched. He toppled over to one side, falling into shadow. Rachel could now see only a vague outline that was shifting and twisting as she watched.

But she could hear the sounds.

Of tearing flesh.

And cracking bones.

And the human cries of pain that shifted into animal whimpers.

The metal chains clattered onto the hard floor, and then there was silence ... except for rapid panting breaths coming from the shadow-shape on the floor.

"Madoc?" Rachel whispered.

The shape moved. And a huge, red-furred, green eyed wolf stepped into the candlelight.

FIFTEEN SHAPES MOVED TOWARDS THE HOUSE, their bellies
low to the ground, ears pricked. They were led by an ancient
silver-furred wolf, who moved slowly, his head turning from
side to side, nostrils flaring, reading the scents on the cool night
air.

There were many humans in the house: five, no, six males
and one female. There were two more males in the grounds.
The wolf scented the bitter gunpowder and oily metal odour
of their weapons.

A red furred, green-eyed female wolf limped up. She was
favouring her left hind paw, and there was a flaking patch of
rust-coloured blood on her fur. She took the lead and led the
wolf pack in a long curve that would bring them in by the back
of the house, around by the stables.

The walkie-talkie on the table crackled with static.

"Two-one to Control. Come in Control."

Detective Inspector Michael Feeney snatched up the radio
and thumbed the Talk switch. "Control to Two-one. Receiving."

*"Movement in the west sector, Sir. A group of twelve or fifteen
individuals. Impossible to make out any further details."*

"Stay sharp." Michael Feeney looked up at Robert and
Elizabeth Stone. "Looks like we're about to have company."
He raised the walkie-talkie again. "All units. Be advised. We
have movement in the west sector. Twelve or fifteen individuals. Do you copy?"

One by one, the four officers in the house, and the two

officers in the grounds, including the officer who had radioed the report, checked in with their call numbers.

"What happens now?" Robert Stone asked tiredly. There were deep shadows under his eyes and the stubble on his face made him look old.

"The house is secure. The servants are being looked after in the local station, so no word of our presence here will leak out. I have four armed men in strategic spots upstairs. Now, we simply wait for our friends out there to get closer and declare their intentions." The inspector smiled and lifted his radio. "Then I'll call in the extra units we've positioned on all the roads. I'll have thirty men here in a matter of minutes, and there'll be two helicopter units in the air. They won't get away. We'll have your daughter back before the dawn," he promised.

Across the fields, a wolf howled.

THE WOLF PADDED ACROSS THE FLOOR and stood before the girl. Its huge green eyes were wide and unblinking, and a thin thread of saliva dripped from its gaping jaws. Razor-sharp pointed teeth glinted.

Rachel's heart was pounding so hard that she was physically trembling in time to its solid beating. She had witnessed the impossible: she had seen the boy turn into a wolf.

The huge animal bent its head, nuzzling at her feet, its nose cold on her flesh. And then its massive jaws snapped shut. When it raised its head, it was holding the remains of the ropes that had bound her legs.

The wave of relief that washed over the girl left her weak. The wolf wasn't going to eat her. But did it still understand her?

"Can you hear me ...?" Her voice was quivering. She coughed and tried again. "Can you hear me?"

The animal tilted its head, pointed ears twitching.

Rachel held out her bound hands. "Free me, please."

The beast moved forward, its breath warm and moist against her hands, and, almost delicately, nipped at the thick rope with its teeth. The cords fell away.

Crouching down, Rachel looked into the wolf's eyes – Madoc's eyes. "What do we do now?" she asked gently. "We're still trapped down here."

The beast's rasping tongue flickered out, touching her cheek, startling her. The wolf then turned away and padded up the stairs, nose close to the old wood. It sniffed all around the door frame, then it stood up on its hind legs, and seemed to be leaning its weight against the wooden door. Finally it turned away and padded back down the stairs.

"There must be a way out of here ..." Rachel began.

Madoc's hind muscles bunched and the dog leapt forward. It struck the middle stair briefly – and then its full weight crashed against the door.

The door collapsed beneath the wolf's weight, the bolts and hinges ripping out of the wall. The noise was incredible, but Rachel didn't wait to see if anyone came to investigate. Slivers of wood were still falling to the floor as she raced up the stairs and stepped out into the hall. The wolf gave a soft bark, turned and headed down the hall to the right. Rachel followed him.

And prayed that she wasn't going to be too late.

Officer Paul Kelly stretched, working his neck from side to side. He was stiff, muscles aching and his toes numb, and there was a raw scratchiness at the back of his throat that he knew meant he was going to have a sore throat in the morning. He rolled over to look back at Seasonstown House. He could see movement behind the lighted windows. It was all right for them. They were warm and dry. They hadn't got the outdoor duty. Right now he needed a large mug of steaming hot coffee, black with two – no, three! – sugars. He reached for his radio and was about to call in, when he remembered that Inspector Feeney had commanded them to keep radio silence unless absolutely necessary ... and Kelly didn't think that calling in for a cup of coffee would be considered absolutely necessary.

Officer Kelly rolled over onto his stomach again, lifted the special night-vision binoculars to his eyes and scanned the horizon. Jimmy, on the lawn on the other side of the house, had reported seeing movement earlier, but Kelly hadn't seen anything. Jimmy had probably been looking at sheep. The night-vision binoculars allowed him to see in the dark by concentrating the available light and then electronically improving the image in the glass. The world was an eerie emerald green, speckled with yellow and white which marked brighter lights; Kelly thought they made everything look like an underwater scene.

He followed the line of the road and then cut across the fields, tracing the hedges. A flicker of movement caught his attention, making him reach for the gun by his side. But then the shape moved again and he realised he was looking at a fox. The fox was trotting almost daintily across the field. Even as he watched, the animal stopped abruptly, head erect, tail rigid. Then it turned and darted into the shelter of thick bushes. Officer Kelly wondered what had startled the animal. Shrugging, he moved the glasses, looking towards the west – when the image was suddenly blotted out as the glasses went blank.

Officer Kelly pulled the glasses away from his eyes – and found himself looking into the face of a nightmare. Huge teeth glinted and before he could even cry out the heavy animal was on top of him. He struck his head hard off the ground and went limp.

The green-eyed wolf caught the man's walkie-talkie in its massive jaws and crushed it in a crackling explosion of sparks. With its belly close to the ground, the wolf slunk closer to the house.

Michael Feeney pressed the Talk button on the walkie-talkie. "Two-one. Any further signs of movement?"

"Negative."

"Two-two. Report." Twenty-two was Officer Paul Kelly's call sign. "Two-two. Are you receiving?"

Crackling silence on the radio.

The young inspector came slowly to his feet. Robert Stone sensed his sudden tension and came to stand by his side.

"Two-two. Are you receiving me?"

There was no reply.

"I think you and Mrs Stone should go up to your bedroom. Lock the door. Open it only for me or Inspector Lanigan."

"It could be a broken radio," Robert Stone suggested.

"It could be," the inspector agreed. "But let's not take any chances."

Robert knelt by the chair where his wife was dozing. When he touched her arm, she awoke with a start. "What's wrong?" she demanded.

"Nothing's wrong. The inspector has suggested we head up to the bedroom. I think he wants us out of the way," he added with a smile. Elizabeth Stone allowed herself to be helped up out of the chair. She knew by the look on her husband's face that something was wrong.

"Try and get some rest," the inspector said as they left the room.

"I doubt it," Elizabeth said with a sad smile.

"Try anyway."

The couple were half way up the stairs when the night was shattered by a burst of gunfire.

"It's started!" Rachel whispered. She stood on the edge of the wood and stared across the fields towards the house. Lights burned in every room, and the house seemed close enough to touch. Madoc loomed up beside her, the moonlight adding to his terrifying appearance. "Come on," she said and ran out of the shelter of the trees, across moon-bright fields towards the distant house. The huge wolf loped silently by her side.

Robert Stone turned the key in the bedroom door, then pushed the heavy wardrobe across it.

Elizabeth was leaning against one of the tall windows,

staring out into the night. "What's happening, Robert? Where's our little girl?" Tears sparkled in her blue eyes. "This is all my fault. You were right, we should have gone away. If we had, none of this would have happened."

Robert wrapped his arms around her, squeezing tightly. He had nothing to say because he knew she was right.

"I'll never forgive myself if anything has happened to Rachel," Elizabeth continued.

"She'll be fine. I'm sure of it," Robert Stone said, but neither he nor his wife believed it.

Inspector Feeney slammed the phone down. He had been trying to call for reinforcements, but the lines were dead. They had obviously been cut. He knew that the walkie-talkie in his hand was only strong enough to broadcast over a short range, but the radio in the car was capable of transmitting to the waiting men. He pressed the Talk button. "Control to all units. We have lost contact with Two-one and Two-two. Phone lines are dead. I am going to the car to call in for back-up. Stay alert."

The inspector checked that his gun was fully loaded and that the safety was off. He stood in the hallway measuring the distance from the door to his car; it couldn't be more than twenty feet, but at that moment, it looked like a mile. He raised his binoculars and scanned the sloping lawn. In the lurid green light of the night-glasses it seemed deserted.

Taking a deep breath, he ran quickly towards the car, desperately hoping he'd left it open. He didn't want to spend precious minutes fumbling for keys. God knows how many people were wandering around the grounds: Two-one had spotted twelve or fifteen people before he'd gone off the air.

The car was open.

Michael Feeney slid into the warm interior with a sigh of relief. Dropping the pistol onto the passenger seat, he snatched the microphone off the dashboard. He was raising it to his lips when he spotted the flicker of movement directly in front of the car. He was still scrambling for the gun when the windscreen exploded and the wolf came in on top of him!

Rachel was squeezing through the hedge when she saw the shape running towards her. For a single moment she though it was Madoc returning, but then she realised that this wolf was bigger, darker. It snarled just as it leapt for her, jaws gaping, white spittle spraying into the air.

Rachel stepped backwards, caught her heel on a root and crashed to the ground. The wolf sailed over her head, so close that she could smell its damp animal odour and feel the heat from its body.

They both came to their feet at the same time. Rachel snatched up her shoe which had fallen off and as the wolf darted in, brought it down hard on the animal's nose. It yelped with surprise and pain, its green eyes watering, and danced back. Rachel turned and ran.

She pounded across the soft ground, elbows tucked in, hands closed into fists, trying to breathe in rhythm with her steps. She could hear the wolf behind her, the scratching of its paws on the earth, its panting breaths. She knew she was going to feel its teeth sink into the flesh of her back or legs.

The ditch she had walked along earlier that day loomed up out of the night. Rachel took it at a jump, bursting through the hedge in a shower of leaves. But the wolf didn't see the ditch; it had its gaze firmly fixed on the girl. With a whine of surprise, it tumbled into the ditch. The girl used the precious seconds to bring her closer to the back of the house. She could hear the horses whinnying nervously in the stables. Her breath was coming in great heaving gasps now, burning in her throat, fire in her lungs. Her legs felt like jelly, and her head was pounding. She risked a quick glance back over her shoulder. The wolf was closing fast, running silently now.

If she could just reach the stables ... get onto a horse ... get a weapon of some sort ...

As she rounded the corner of the stables, a wolf padded out into the centre of the courtyard and stood in the moonlight facing her. Rachel skidded to a halt and looked back. The second wolf was almost on top of her. When she looked up again, the first wolf was racing towards her. She screamed once as both beasts leapt at her.

ROBERT STONE SAT BOLT UPRIGHT. "That was Rachel," he said aloud. He looked at his wife. "Didn't you hear the scream?"

She shook her head slowly. "I heard nothing."

"It was Rachel," he repeated. He ran to the window and peered out, but he could see nothing ... and then he realised that he could hear nothing either. No crackling radio, no movement of the other police officers in the house, no clattering footsteps or muffled shouts. Crossing to the door, he pushed away the wardrobe, and turned the key in the lock.

"Robert! Where are you going?" Elizabeth demanded.

He ignored the question. "Lock the door behind me," he said, and stepped out onto the landing.

Ten of the largest wolves he'd ever seen in his life – green-eyed, red-furred – were padding up the stairs. The pack leader opened its mouth and howled. The sound was deafening in the confines of the house, echoing and re-echoing off the marble floor. It sounded like an evil human laugh.

The wolf sailed right over Rachel's head, crashing into the beast that had been following her. Both animals went down in a snarling tangle of fur.

"Madoc," the girl breathed. She pressed herself up against the stable walls, hearing the frightened whickering of the horses in their stalls, her gaze riveted on the fighting wolves.

The animals rolled around on the ground, biting and clawing at one another. As they tumbled across the stable yard in the moonlight, Rachel caught the flickering image of Madoc fighting with an older, taller boy, but then the image vanished and she could only see the wolves. The slightly smaller wolf – Madoc, she thought – finally managed to roll the larger beast over and lock its jaws around the other's throat. It started shaking the bigger dog from side to side. There was a sudden cracking snap and the wolf went limp. Madoc tossed the still body into the shadows.

The victorious wolf trotted up to Rachel. There was blood on its teeth, but it hadn't come out of the fight without a scratch. Part of its left ear was bent and bleeding and there was a long wound across its chest. It nuzzled at her hand, licking it. Rachel knelt and hugged the animal. "We've got to get my parents out of the house," she whispered, "but how are going to get past the wolves?"

The wolf's mouth worked, a combination of whimpers and tiny barks combining to form a single word: "Fire."

Robert Stone slammed the door shut behind him and turned the key with trembling fingers ... just as the first of the wolves hit the wood. Although the door didn't break, the force of the blow was enough to send him staggering back. He threw himself against the door, while Elizabeth struggled to push the heavy wardrobe into place. When she'd got it close enough, Robert caught it, pulling it into position. "What's out there?" she whispered.

"Wolves," Robert whispered. "Wolves!" he repeated, as if he didn't believe it.

"There are no wolves in Ireland," Elizabeth said shakily.

The wolf pack outside the door began howling triumphantly. And then, in blow after blow, the bedroom door was slowly torn apart.

"Where are the police?" Elizabeth demanded.

Robert shuddered. "The wolves must have got them." Tears sprang to his eyes. "They must have got Rachel too."

Madoc jumped through the kitchen window, shattering it into hundreds of flying shards. Rachel climbed through the opening, hissing in pain as she sliced the palm of her hand on a sliver of glass. They could hear a solid banging sound from upstairs.

While Madoc stood guard at the door, the girl searched through the cupboards beneath the sink, pulling out pots and pans, looking for something inflammable. She finally came across a dozen bottles of cooking oil. She lifted one of the plastic bottles, squeezing it slightly, wondering if it would burn. In another cupboard, she discovered piles of old newspapers, fire lighters and matches. She also pulled out two big packages of sugar.

Rachel spread the newspapers around the room and then sprinkled them with the cooking oil. She broke open a packet of fire lighters and scattered them onto the newspapers, then added the sugar. There was a chip-pan on the shelf beneath the sink. Rachel tipped it over, allowing foul-smelling grease to puddle thickly on the newspapers. She finally lifted an old-fashioned long-haired broom and dipped it into the oily mess on the floor, until the head was thickly coated with grease. Finally she turned on the gas cooker and oven, blinking sudden tears as the foul gas stung her eyes.

"Ready?" she asked Madoc. The wolf didn't reply.

Rachel eased open the kitchen door. The noise from upstairs was louder now, and she could identify the sound of cracking wood. She could also hear her parents muffled shouts and cries.

Propping the sweeping brush up against the door, Rachel lifted the box of long kitchen matches. She was surprised by how calm she felt as she pushed open the box and shook out a match. Then, on impulse, she tossed the remainder across the floor.

The match caught first time, the bitter sharp odour of sulphur wiping away the sickly sweet smell of the oil and the heavier stink of the gas. Taking a deep breath, she tossed the match onto the floor ... .

The explosion lifted her up and threw her almost the full length of the hall.

Dazed and bruised, Rachel rolled over onto her hands and knees, crouching while the world spun madly around her. Madoc padded up to her, smoke coiling off his fur, carrying the sweeping brush in his mouth. The handle had snapped in half. Catching hold of the hair around his neck, Rachel came stiffly to her feet. Smoke and flames were pouring out of the kitchen. The fire had splashed the oil down the length of the hall and across the walls where it hung in long burning streaks. The flames were rapidly eating their way along the skirting-board. The house filled with noise – a mixture of the fire's roaring crackle and the confused and frightened howling of the wolves.

The girl lifted the broken-handled sweeping brush and plunged its head into a burning newspaper. The head of the brush popped alight. Holding the brush before her like a sword, Rachel Stone advanced up the stairs.

The sudden thump of the explosion knocked Robert and Elizabeth Stone to the floor. "What was that?" Elizabeth whispered.

But before Robert could answer, they smelt the smoke, and then the terrifying sound of burning timber.

"Fire!" Robert breathed. He picked up the bedside locker and heaved it through the nearest window. It seemed to fall a long way before it shattered in the courtyard below. He helped his wife through the broken frame onto the little balcony. They were separated from the next balcony by a gap of no more than four feet. Robert pointed out a route. "It's an easy jump. Go from balcony to balcony to that point there, swing down, and drop into that room – whatever it is. And whatever you do – don't look down."

"What about you?" Elizabeth demanded.

"I'll be right behind you," he promised.

There was a high-pitched crack as the bedroom door split. The mirror on the front of the wardrobe shattered with the force of the blow.

Without thinking, Elizabeth Stone leaped across the gap onto the next balcony. She fell heavily onto her hands and knees, cutting them on the metal railing.

Robert was climbing onto the rail when the wardrobe toppled to the floor, and six of the huge wolves poured into the room.

Four of the wolves moved down the stairs towards Rachel and Madoc. One of them was the old pack leader, moving slowly, almost stiffly. The wolf stopped and stared at Rachel.

And then it changed.

The transformation was far smoother than Madoc's. One moment it had been a wolf, the next its muscles had rippled beneath its fur and the beast was rising up on its hind paws, which were lengthening, growing, straightening, while its forepaws were twisting, bent and claw-like long-nailed fingers growing out of what had been wolf's pads. His elongated snout pulled back with the sound of breaking bone, the bristles on his face withdrawing into the skin.

And it was Piers de Courtney.

But the transformation was not entirely successful. Now he was something between man and wolf, the body of a man but twisted into an animal-like posture, his face still with the dog-like skull beneath a human skin. In that moment he resembled a creature from nightmare: he was a true werewolf.

He smiled at Rachel, showing long ragged teeth. "Two hundred and more years ago, I became one of the clan of Natalis in this house. It is fitting that it should be in this house that I should give up that terrible affliction." He reached for Rachel with his filthy talons. "I was going to pass on the curse to your mother and father – and then all of my clan would have tasted their blood and been made human. But you – we never had any intention of changing you. Maeve wanted to eat you, but I decided you would be my bride."

Without saying a word, Rachel swung the burning brush at the werewolf. Its sudden movement caught him by surprise and he staggered backwards. The three wolves behind him moved forward then, snapping and snarling at the girl, but she drove them back with the fire, singeing fur and burning flesh.

"Mom? Dad!" Rachel shouted. She coughed as smoke tickled the back of her throat. She saw movement beyond the shattered door of her parents' bedroom, and she experienced a sudden wave of relief ... until six of the wolves appeared in the ruined doorway. They stood at the top of the stairs and then, slowly ... slowly ... they began to move downwards.

Piers de Courtney was on his feet again. The old man looked even more wolf-like now, and coarse reddish hair had begun sprouting in his cheeks.

"Your parents are gone," he panted. "They have fled. So that only leaves you. But one is enough for my plan. Perhaps you will never be my bride, but you will carry the curse of the clan of Natalis." He bared his teeth, threw back his head and howled.

Rachel took a step back down the stairs ... and another ... and another, her eyes flicking amongst the wolves, knowing that one of them would make a move. Madoc came around to stand by her side, teeth bared in a silent growl.

"And when we are finished with you," de Courtney continued, "and you are wolf and we are human, perhaps we shall feast off the traitor, Madoc. I understand dogmeat is considered a delicacy in some parts of the world." He pointed. "Take them!"

Rachel turned and ran ... and the stairs vanished beneath her feet.

She was unconscious for less than a minute. When she awoke she was lying trapped beneath a lattice-work of timbers, in the space under the stairs. The fire raged all around her, the smoke clinging and deadly. It took her a few moments to work out what had happened. The fire had eaten through the stair supports, and the combined weight of all the wolves had caused them to cave in.

She shielded her eyes as pieces of burning wood toppled down, cinders and sparks singeing her cheeks, scorching her flesh. There was a musical crash almost overhead, and she realised that the chandelier in the hall had fallen and exploded across the marble tiles.

The girl attempted to pull herself free, but her legs were trapped beneath the wooden stair beams. Sitting up, she pushed at the nearest length of wood, but it didn't budge.

Stay calm. Stay calm.

She could wriggle her toes and flex the muscles in her thighs and calves, so she didn't think there was anything broken. All she had to do was move one large piece of wood and one smaller one, and she should be able to slide free. She pulled at the nearest piece, burning her hands as she attempted to drag it away. It wouldn't budge.

Stay calm. Stay calm.

A sudden curl of white smoke sent her into a spasm of coughing. Half-twisting, she realised that the fire was now taking hold behind her ... no, beneath her! The fire in the kitchen must have burned through into the cellars. She heard a series of rattling pops, and then the sudden roar of intense heat, as the flames ate through the bottles of alcohol in the wine cellar.

"Stay calm," she hissed fiercely as she struggled to free herself, but she succeeding only in creating a minor avalanche of burnt wood and plasterboard.

Fire snapped alight across from her, illuminating the darkness beneath the stairs. And now she could see the scattered bodies of the werewolves. When the stairs had caved in, they had fallen in too, their backs crushed by the timbers.

The girl smiled grimly. "The curse ends tonight," she whispered.

There was movement overhead, dirt trickling down onto her hair. Rachel looked up ... but her shout of relief turned to one of terror. A wolf's head poked over the edge. Even without the flickering transformation that altered its head for a moment, making it a mixture of dog and girl, Rachel recognised Maeve.

The wolf howled triumphantly and dropped the fifteen feet to land lightly beside the trapped girl, jaws gaping, saliva drooling onto its fur.

"No!" Rachel shook her head slightly; it wasn't going to end like this, not trapped and eaten by a savage werewolf. Her fingers touched a piece of charred wood. She brought it around in a quick movement, catching the wolf across the shoulder, snapping the wood in half, knocking the beast off-balance. As the wolf came to its feet, it knocked aside a piece of board ... and revealed the body of Piers de Courtney still locked in its wolf-man shape. For a moment, Maeve lost control and the were-change flickered through her features, making her – like de Courtney – half wolf, half human. Throwing back her head, she howled, a long, terrifying wail of sorrow and despair.

When she turned back to Rachel the were-change hadn't completely changed her. Her body was that of a huge red-furred wolf, but her face was recognisably human.

"I will kill you tonight," Maeve whispered hoarsely, her voice raw and rasping. Whatever else she said was lost as the fire roared up through the house. Smoke began curling up from the floor at Maeve's feet, and Rachel could feel the heat from the fire raging in the cellars seeping up through the floor. It would give way at any moment, plunging them both into the inferno below. Maeve howled again, a long triumphant cry and launched herself at Rachel ... and a wolf dropped down onto the beast's back, sinking its teeth into the creature's neck.

"Madoc," Rachel breathed.

The two wolves struggled together. The girl could hear snarling, mingled with what sounded like muffled shouts and curses. Flaming timbers crashed down on top of the fighting animals, noxious black and grey smoke was now seeping up through every floorboard. She couldn't breathe, couldn't see. The heat from the burning cellars blistered her flesh.

Maeve managed to throw off her brother once, and then lunged towards Rachel, jaws gaping. Madoc caught her by the tail just as her teeth were about to close into Rachel's outstretched arm and dragged her back.

A flame danced across the floor. And then another. And another. Suddenly a whole section of the wooden floor blackened and burst into flame. The wolves separated as the flames leapt up between them ... and then the floor gave way, plummeting one of the wolves into the flaming cellar below. The remaining wolf turned it glowing green eyes on Rachel. Its left ear was bent.

"Madoc," she breathed, throwing her arms around his neck. Then the smoke coiled around her and she remembered no more.

Sunday, 1st November

MYSTERY BLAZE GUTS HISTORIC HOUSE

Police and local fire officers are treating as "suspicious" a mystery fire which destroyed historic Seasonstown House, just outside Kildare.

The fire, which experts believe started in the kitchens, may have claimed the lives of several police officers who were investigating threats to the present owners of the house, Mr & Mrs Stone, the owners of the prestigious Stone Stables.

Robert and Elizabeth Stone managed to escape by climbing through a bedroom window. Reports that Rachel Stone (15), was dragged from the blazing house by a large dog were dismissed as "nonsense" by Robert Stone.

Mr and Mrs Stone said they were returning to California with their daughter, at the earliest opportunity. Rachel Stone is recovering from minor cuts and burns and the effects of smoke inhalation in the Blackrock Clinic, Dublin.

One month later

Epilogue

RACHEL STONE LEANED AGAINST THE WINDOWSILL and stared down at the beach. The moon was high in a clear sky, painting the sea black and silver, turning the beach to shimmering speckles. She could hear the sound of the surf on the shore, hissing and sighing like some great sea-creature breathing gently.

Tomorrow she would go surfing.

She turned away from the window and climbed into bed, feeling the silk sheets cool and smooth beneath her skin. It felt good to be home in California. The nightmares had stopped too. Now, less than four weeks after the terrifying events in Ireland, everything was beginning to blur, and she found it hard to distinguish between what had really happened and what she thought had happened. She also realised that there were parts that she would never want to remember.

Had she really seen a man change into a wolf?

And Madoc. What had happened to the boy ... and the dog?

When she'd finally been able to answer the question her parents and the police had asked, she'd simply told them that she had been kidnapped, but managed to escape. She never mentioned the wolves. She'd learned that the police had found the derelict building in the nearby wood. She'd also read the report in the newspaper which said that she had been pulled from the burning house by a huge dog. When she asked her father about that report, he had looked away and denied it. But she knew he was lying. He had never spoken about the wolves that had torn his bedroom door off its hinges.

Rachel lifted her arm and looked at the neat semi-circular

cut just below the elbow. She had puzzled over it for a while, wondering how she had got it ... until she realised that she was looking at teeth marks. This was where Madoc had caught her, to pull her from the burning house. Now it was nothing more than a thin red line. She traced the scar with her finger; it would fade soon.

Her nail scraped the flesh.

Rachel frowned. She had cut her nails earlier that day, spending an hour sitting on the porch, idly watching the people playing on the beach below. Spreading her hands, she looked at her splayed fingers. Her nails were long!

Her skin itched. She scratched the back of her hand ... and then realised that she was scratching coarse hair!

The girl sat bolt upright in the bed as the realisation struck her. Long twisting hairs were appearing on the backs of her hands, growing as she watched.

And the hair was red, blood red.

With the sound of snapping wood, her fingers were lengthening, the knuckles and joints thickening, twisting her hands into paws, tipped with razor-sharp claws ...

Rachel Stone opened her mouth and howled.

GEMINI GAME

Michael Scott

BJ and Liz O'Connor are gamemakers, but when their virtual reality computer game *Night's Castle* develops a bug, they risk their lives to try to solve the problem. An exciting futuristic novel.

HOUSE OF THE DEAD

Michael Scott

Something goes very wrong when Claire and Patrick go to Newgrange on their school tour. Can they find a way to keep the evil powers they have released from destroying the whole of Ireland?

MOONLIGHT

Michael Carroll

Moonlight is not just an ordinary horse. His owner dreams he will be the fastest racehorse ever. But Cathy intervenes, and the result is a tense, nail-biting chase for survival.